BETWEEN WORLDS 9

RHYTHMS SHARED

LORI WOLF-HEFFNER

HEAD IN THE GROUND PUBLISHING

To Heather Wright, my high school English teacher who years later became my editor and mentor. Thank you, Heather, for helping this series fly.

CHAPTER ONE

*J*uliana rushed with the lunch dishes toward the sink, where Mom was running hot water. The dishwasher had already been loaded with plates, cutlery, and glasses and turned on. They just needed to wash the serving dishes.

Dad laughed. "I don't think I've ever seen you this excited about cleaning the kitchen."

Opa, sitting at the table beside Dad, his eyes bright with amusement, agreed.

Juliana stopped for a moment and crossed her arms. "I don't get it. You make fun of me when I'm too slow *and* when I'm too fast. What's the right speed?"

"One day, when you're a parent," Dad said, "you'll understand."

Mom rubbed her daughter's shoulder. "Paul, no one has

to be a parent." She spoke to Juliana. "Of course we know why you're so excited."

Dad and Opa passed the last of the dishes to Juliana to carry to the sink.

"I can't wait to see Rachel and Rhys either," Dad said.

Although Juliana and Rachel had been talking several times a week since Juliana moved from Calgary to Kitchener in the winter, this would be the first time they'd see each other in person. Juliana's insides were churning with excitement. She had already confirmed with Rachel and her cousin Sophie that they'd meet this afternoon after Rachel's father dropped her off and returned to Toronto for his business meetings. Then Juliana's best friend and her best cousin could finally get to know each other. And, later this week, Juliana and Rachel would be dancing together at the studio!

Plus, I can show her Elisabeth's drawings in person, Juliana thought.

She glanced at the clock in the kitchen and jumped. "Their plane just landed in Toronto!"

"Whose plane?" Opa asked, and Juliana caught Mom's look of concern.

"Rachel and her father are visiting today." Juliana explained the situation to Opa as though it were new information for him. She'd learned that asking Alzheimer's patients questions like "Don't you remember?" not only did nothing for their memory, but it also made them feel worse about their condition. "Rachel will stay here in the guest bedroom, and Rhys—her father—has meetings all week in Toronto."

Opa smiled. "She's your best friend from Calgary, right?"

Juliana nodded.

"You're happy to meet her, Yulika!"

Another thing Juliana had noticed was new mistakes in Opa's English. Mom had explained to her that his native German seemed to be encroaching on his English more than it used to. Although he'd always had an accent and used some German nicknames—which was why he called her "Yulika"—she, too, had detected that he was making more errors.

"She's very much looking forward to it, Tata," Mom said, politely correcting him.

Dad stood up and glanced at his watch. "That means they'll be here in about two hours. I have time to take the car in."

Right before Rachel and Rhys were to arrive? The engine had been making rumbling noises for a few days. Couldn't he help out with the housework a little?

Not only was there housework, but Juliana had homework for her summer class.

"You can't do dishes?" she asked. "Then I can get started on this report for school."

"What's it on?" Mom asked.

"Career investigation. It's due next Monday, and I have to admit, I'm kind of stuck."

Mom dried a platter. "We can talk about it while we do dishes, if you want."

Juliana sighed. She preferred to think it through alone for many reasons, the first of which was that she didn't know where to start. Unlike some of the others in her online class who seemed to know exactly what they wanted to study out of high school, Juliana had no idea.

Dad grabbed his keys from the counter. "I need to get this in today. But once you learn how to drive, you can be the person to take it in."

Juliana sighed.

Opa shook his head and laughed at the scene playing out before him. "In Mammi's time, you learned to drive a wagon before you were a teenager. If you were a boy. But Mammi learned while her *tata* was away. She told me all the time that her *mammi* never approved. But Georg taught her so she could help her family more."

"Sounds like freedom." Juliana put on rubber gloves.

"Sure," Mom said, "if you want a vehicle that leaves piles of poop right in front of you while you ride."

Juliana had to laugh at that one.

After Dad left, Opa announced he was going to go for a walk.

"Don't stray too far, Tata," Mom said.

"I know, I know." He pointed to his head. "Roof*schaden*."

After he left, Mom sighed. Usually Opa would call his Alzheimer's either roof damage or *dachschaden*. "I'm worried about him. His walks are longer and longer these days, and he is really mixing up his languages."

Juliana shared Mom's concern. She'd also read recently that getting lost and losing track of time were symptoms of advancing Alzheimer's. She'd said nothing to Mom out of fear for worrying her more, but it looked like Mom was already worrying.

To their relief, Opa returned a mere half hour later and headed to the basement to watch TV. By the time Dad returned an hour later, Juliana had completed her cleaning and had even had time to do some school work.

Of course, the anticipation of what was going to be the best week of her year hindered her concentration, so nothing really got done.

Then the doorbell rang at last.

Juliana raced to the side door, almost tripping down the two stairs to the landing.

She flung the door open. Before her stood her best friend, tears already in her eyes and wearing the biggest smile Juliana had seen in ages.

Without saying a word, they wrapped their arms around each other and held on tight.

CHAPTER TWO

*E*lisabeth saw Stefan opening the first gate on her property. Her heart started to flutter and her palms began to sweat. She rubbed her hands on her dark-blue apron to settle both problems.

Stefan waved to his friend Georg, who was crouched by the chicken coop with Elisabeth's brother, Luki, showing him how to fix a fence. Georg waved back. Luki, though, didn't notice as he was concentrating so he didn't hit his finger with the hammer.

Stefan laughed at the sight as he strolled through the second gate, then past the ducks and the geese, and then the chicken coop. Then he looked at Elisabeth with a smile.

"Stefan," Elisabeth said. "It's nice to see you." Did that sound too formal? Oh no. Was she acting strange? Things between her and Stefan had changed in recent weeks, and Elisabeth didn't understand what those changes meant.

Stefan doffed his cap as he walked up to her. "I've done my work at the church for the day, so I thought I'd drop by to see if I can help with anything here, since Herr Schuhmacher is coming home soon."

Tata had travelled to America last November—ten months ago—to earn more money for the family. He had planned to stay in America for a year so that he could earn enough money to replace their house's thatch roof with a modern one and save for a dowry for Elisabeth, who was old enough to get married. Tata had written to explain that he was coming home sooner than planned, but he had not said why.

"That's very kind of you." Elisabeth's heart fluttered again as she lowered the bucket into the well. "But I'm just about to wash dishes."

Stefan raised an eyebrow. "And a man can't help?"

Elisabeth blinked. She'd never seen a man wash dishes. Was he offering to help? Or...? Elisabeth didn't know what could come after "or." Men didn't wash dishes.

She placed both of her hands on the handle of the well to reel the full bucket back up, but Stefan gently pushed her out of the way and grasped the handle with his left hand. He'd lost his right arm just past the elbow in the war that had almost torn Europe apart. "Let me help." He cranked the handle and raised the bucket.

"Thank you." Elisabeth unhooked the pail, turned around, and bumped right into Luki, who stood behind her, his hammer in hand. The pail emptied all over her, drenching her to the bone with cold water. "Luki!"

Luki laughed at his sister.

Elisabeth tried to wring out her apron so she didn't have to make eye contact with Stefan. She knew her cheeks were cherry red. "Luki. You apologize right now!"

Luki stuck out his tongue and turned on his heel, only to be met by Georg's towering figure.

Unlike Elisabeth, who often had to resort to bribes to get her young brother to do anything, Georg only had to look at him.

Luki turned around and mumbled an apology.

"Louder," Georg said gently.

"I'm sorry for knocking the pail over. I wanted to show you my hammer. Georg made it just for me."

That was indeed a special gift. Georg's father—Tata's brother—had passed away the month before, leaving Georg in charge of his blacksmithing workshop. Georg's wife, Eva, had just given birth to their first child, Little Konrad. Georg was very busy these days, so the gift was a kindness.

"Thank you for taking so much time," Elisabeth said to her cousin.

Stefan grasped the hammer, tossed it in the air, and caught it again. "This is excellent work, Georg," he said.

"It's weighted really well." He flipped the hammer and passed it back to Luki, handle first. "You take care of this, Luki. This is very special."

Luki darted back to the coop to continue his work.

Georg gave a gentle smile at Elisabeth's wet clothes. "I suppose you can't make him wash your clothes."

She shook her head. "Mammi would yell at me for tricking him into doing my work and taking him away from his."

"I'll make sure he gives the horse stall an extra sweeping." Georg excused himself and returned to showing Luki the tasks that men did.

"Why don't you go inside to change," Stefan said, "and I'll fill your wash basins for you."

Elisabeth thanked him and went inside. She could probably just hang her clothing out to dry: it wasn't particularly dirty, and it had just been splashed with clean water.

Back outside in almost no time, Elisabeth went to the open kitchen behind the house to begin washing lunch dishes. She stopped, her mouth agape: Anna and Rosina had already begun with the washing.

"That's right," Stefan said. "Make sure you get all that dirt off."

Why did her siblings all listen better to men than women?

Elisabeth approached the basins, but Stefan shook his

head. "I can keep an eye on them. I'm sure you have garden work or other chores."

Why was Elisabeth's heart pounding? Yes, she had grown fond of Stefan over the six months or so they'd gotten to know each other. Not only did she admire his kind heart, but the persistence he showed in trying to find work despite his injury demonstrated an unusual kind of courage. Stefan had once told her that, on his travels back from Russia after the war, he had seen former soldiers wearing nothing but their uniforms—they didn't have any other clothing—begging in the streets because no one would take them in. Not even their own families.

Elisabeth couldn't figure out how all these people refused to help, as Jesus said, the least fortunate among them. Stefan was not like that. Stefan was always ready to help, even if it meant helping with women's work.

"Thank you," she replied. "You're very kind."

With time running out to prepare the household for Tata's arrival, Stefan's help had come at the right moment. Elisabeth knew she might only have one more chance to draw in her sketchbook before Tata returned. He had given her the book so she could draw everything important that had happened while he'd been gone.

She couldn't wait to show it to him.

CHAPTER THREE

Mr. Casimiro stopped by the girls' table, dirty dishes in hand.

"How is it?" he asked.

Sophie sipped on her chocolate milkshake. Juliana enjoyed her fruit flan.

Rachel was downing a full vanilla sundae. "Jules said the food here was good. I had no idea it was *this* good." She shoved another spoonful in her mouth as Juliana and Sophie laughed.

"I'm glad to hear it!" He headed toward the kitchen.

Casimiro's was their first stop. The café had been located in the Belmont Village shopping strip for thirty or forty years. It had a bit of a 1950s appeal to it, with a pink, black, white, and chrome colour scheme. And Casimiro's was only a two-minute walk for Juliana and Sophie.

"It's so awesome to finally introduce you two to each other. Now my summer is complete. I just wish I didn't have summer school in the way."

Rachel paused with her next spoonful in front of her mouth. "I'm glad Dad let me come along on his business trip, and your parents are okay with me staying with you."

"Of course they are!" Juliana said.

"I can't wait to check out that market outside," Sophie said. "Maybe you'll find something that reminds you of Kitchener to take home with you, Rachel."

"I just might!"

"How's summer school going, anyway?" Sophie asked Juliana. "I'd hate to have to go to school in the summer."

"Yeah. But it was the only way to transition from my school system in Calgary to the one here."

"It's a course about careers?" Rachel asked.

"For two weeks. Then civics for two weeks. Right now, I have to do this career project. Mom thinks it'll be good for me, but having to figure out what I want to do for the rest of my life is *a lot* of pressure."

Rachel stared thoughtfully at her ice cream. "Do you have to know? Or can you just use this project to explore options?"

"That depends." Juliana reminded her friend that some professions, like surgeon, needed so much time to study that it helped to know what you wanted to do when you were in high school.

"True," Rachel said, her mouth full. "Although I don't see you as a surgeon. But there are lots of other jobs that can take many years of study. Teachers, engineers, researchers of any kind…"

"And then there are *so* many careers I'd never thought of. Someone has to drive a train, right? Or work the control tower of an airport. Or repair buses."

Mr. Casimiro walked by, his arms full of plates. "I certainly didn't know when I was your age that I'd immigrate to Canada and open a restaurant. I was training with my grandfather to be a fishmonger."

Sophie tilted her head to the side. "A what?"

"A fishmonger. Someone who catches and sells fish. We lived in a coastal village in Portugal." Without saying more, he walked off, probably because the plates were heavy.

"So, Mr. Casimiro didn't have to plan his whole life when he was a kid," Juliana said.

Sophie sipped thoughtfully for a moment. "I don't think that's entirely true. He said he was *learning* how to be a fishmonger when he was our age. So, he had career plans."

Mr. Casimiro, returning with a cloth and spray bottle, chuckled. "I wouldn't call those career plans. You just did what someone in your family did. I was free labour while I was learning, and I'd have a job for life when I was old enough. What you kids have to do these days to get a job…" He shook his head. "I'm happy I'm not your age." He wiped down the table he'd just cleared and then moved on to other tasks.

"He does have a point," Sophie said. "All I know is that I don't want to be a mom to six kids." Juliana knew Sophie was thinking of her mother. Sophie was the second youngest of Aunt Anne's six children.

"And I don't want to manage a grocery store," Juliana said. "It sounds like Mom just deals with complaints all day. And suppliers who don't deliver on time."

"You used to love joining your dad on his day trips trucking," Rachel said.

Juliana felt a moment of sadness as she remembered all the years her father had worked as a trucker, often gone for a week or longer. Yes, those day trips were highlights of her childhood, but truth be told, she'd have happily given them up if it had meant her father had been home every evening.

"No. You miss your friends and family too much. So, I guess train engineer is out, too." Juliana pulled out her phone and called up her assignment. "We're supposed to interview three people about their jobs, and they can't be family. But I'm still new here. Who can I ask? And who would talk to a kid they don't know?"

Juliana ran her finger along the edge of the table. "And, I love dance, but I can't see myself auditioning all the time to earn money and then starting again in a new career in my thirties or forties."

Sophie sat back in her chair, thinking again. "You love our great-grandmother's stories."

Juliana deliberated for a moment. "I love the stories, but I hate writing essays, and I can't memorize dates to save my life."

They finished their food, and Mr. Casimiro brought them their bills.

"How did you end up owning a restaurant?" Juliana asked as she paid with her debit card. She might as well start her project somewhere.

He smiled. "My wife knew how to cook, and I knew how to be friendly. We had some savings, and the rest we borrowed from friends and extended family—banks don't like lending to new immigrants." He handed Juliana her receipt and passed the debit machine to Sophie.

Sophie looked a little to the side as she punched in her code. She had Stargardt disease, a rare condition that caused young people to lose their central vision. It meant she couldn't see the numbers if she looked straight at them.

"But you could've, I don't know, opened another kind of business, right? Or worked for someone?"

Casimiro accepted the machine back from Sophie. "With our own business, my wife and I could bring the kids to work, teach them how to work, and set our own hours." He handed Sophie her receipt and let out a dry laugh. "Of course, the government takes every second penny. We didn't expect that." He shrugged. "But we figured out how to make it work." He handed Juliana her receipt and passed the machine to Rachel. "Why are you so interested? Do you want to run a restaurant someday?"

Juliana shook her head and explained the project as Rachel tapped her debit card and waited for the receipt.

"I see." Mr. Casimiro thought for a moment. "Some of the shop owners in Belmont Village have had very interesting careers." He pointed outside. "Pauline, the owner of Claire's Tea Shop, was a mascot actor. If you see a tall purple cat walking around outside at today's market, that's her."

Rachel's eyes grew large. "A mascot? That'd be so cool!"

But Juliana wrinkled her nose. Dressing up like a stuffed toy was not her idea of a career.

Mr. Casimiro noticed her reaction and laughed. "I know it sounds silly. We laugh at mascots in Europe. Here..." He took a piece of paper from the pocket of his apron and wrote on it before handing it to Juliana. "Pauline Robinson, Perry, Toronto Peregrines. Look her up. She was in the newspaper maybe two years ago. Very interesting. I had no idea, and I've known Claire, her mother, for decades."

Juliana had met Claire the month before. The kindly older woman had actually known their relative Georg Schuhmacher—who had gone by George Shoemaker here in Canada—and therefore had helped Juliana unlock the true story of how the Schuhmachers had landed in Canada. But Juliana didn't know Claire's daughter.

He tapped on the table. "Do talk to Pauline. Even if you don't want to dress up in costumes like that, she would be good to talk to. She's met so many interesting people. She even got to shake the prime minister's hand."

Well, maybe...

Juliana thanked Mr. Casimiro for his advice and they prepared to leave.

But no sooner were they standing outside the diner than a purple cat walking on two legs came toward them, a creepy smile sewn on its plush face, and its arms wide open as kids ran in for a hug. Sophie pulled Juliana toward the costumed character.

"Oh my god, no, Sophie. Just no." She pulled her arm away. "Why anyone would do that and be proud of it... ugh!"

Sophie playfully but indignantly parked her hands on her hips. "She sounds like a cool person. You're going to tell me you didn't hug your favourite cartoon characters when you were a kid?"

"Well, sure, yeah..."

"Forget it, Sophie," Rachel said. "Mascot work isn't for Juliana. She absolutely hates improvisation. Actually, she hates any kind of change."

Juliana rolled her eyes.

"It's true!" Rachel insisted. "You even hated the surprise farewell party we threw for you."

Sophie's eyes opened wide. "She did?"

"She tried to hide it when we all shouted, 'Surprise!' But I saw it."

Juliana crossed her arms and narrowed her eyes. Rachel was laughing openly at her, although Sophie was at least trying to hold in her amusement.

"I like to plan," Juliana said. "Nothing wrong with that. Now. We had *planned* to look at these different stands. So, let's go."

Juliana tried to keep a serious expression on her face, but her best friend and favourite cousin were still smiling. Eventually, Juliana gave in and smiled, too.

The three girls began walking from tent to tent, checking out different items for sale, like jewellery, cutting boards, stickers, soaps, and more.

After shopping at the market, they headed back to Juliana's home, each with a handmade bracelet now adorning their wrist. But no sooner had Juliana unlocked the side door than they heard Mom's raised voice coming from the laundry room in the basement.

"Tata! I told you! I had no idea that was in there!"

"It was my only one! You have to be better careful when you wash my clothes!"

The argument continued, sometimes with Opa slipping into German and Mom replying in English.

The three girls exchanged concerned glances.

"Should I go down there?" Juliana asked.

Sophie shook her head. "Never get involved in a fight between Opa and our moms."

Juliana obviously had a few things to learn. "To my room?"

The others agreed.

The three girls tried to ignore the raised voices from the basement, but the floors and walls in this old house were paper thin, so they heard everything.

Eventually, a door downstairs slammed, and a moment later, they heard footsteps head into Juliana's parents' bedroom.

"What do you think happened?" Sophie whispered. "I didn't understand the German."

"Me neither," Juliana replied.

Rachel shrugged. "My best guess would be that something got damaged in the wash."

Juliana pointed to the wall of her parents' bedroom. "I think I should..."

"Rachel and I will check the laundry room," Sophie said. "If Opa comes in, I'll say I left something there."

Their plan of attack in place, they split up.

Juliana knocked on Mom's door.

"Just a second!" Mom was attempting to sound cheery, but Juliana wasn't fooled.

Mom opened the door. Her mascara was smudged. Juliana didn't know where to start.

"It's fine," Mom said. "He just had another one of his anger outbursts." She sighed. "They've become more frequent lately. We see his neurologist Thursday, so that's a start."

But this time was different: Mom had been crying. "What was he angry about?"

Mom sighed and sat down on her bed.

"I'm usually really good with checking your grandfather's pockets before I do the wash. Nothing worse than scraps of Kleenex everywhere." She let out a dry laugh. "But this time...this time, I was on the phone dealing with work, and I didn't check." Her tears returned and she wiped them away. Juliana handed her mom the box of tissues from her nightstand. Mom dabbed at her eyes and blew her nose.

"I had no idea that Tata carried a small photo of his mother in his pocket every day."

Juliana's jaw dropped. "He has a photo of Elisabeth? And he never said anything?"

"Had," Mom corrected. "It went through the wash and now it's in pieces." Mom started to cry again. "I didn't know."

Juliana gave her mom a hug. She hadn't known either. Why hadn't Opa said anything?

"Turns out he always took the photo out before he put his pants in the wash." Mom sniffled. "He forgot this time and says he doesn't have another one."

Juliana tried to comfort Mom. "But there's that drawer

of photos. And Aunt Anne has a bunch of photo albums. Surely, there must be another photo somewhere?"

Mom shrugged. "He may have shown me when I was young...but it's not like I cared then." She took a deep breath and let it out. "All I know about her is that she had a hard life...and then whatever you've been able to find out. I never really thought to ask those kinds of questions and we lived so far away."

"Would Uncle Peter recognize her?"

Mom sighed. She pulled her phone from her pants pocket. "I'd better call Annie and Peter and let them know what happened, in case he calls them in a panic."

Juliana took that as her cue to leave. At least she had the story.

Rachel and Sophie were already back sitting on her bed when she returned to her room.

Sophie held open her hand. "We found this."

There it was: the photo in pieces. Juliana could have been able to see her great-grandmother's face had she known there was a photograph of Elisabeth. She had come to see her great-grandmother as a friend after discovering her drawings. She gingerly touched the frayed, damp pieces.

"We need to find Opa a new picture of her."

CHAPTER FOUR

"That man is not right in the head," Mammi said to Elisabeth as they used their pitchforks to turn the huge compost-and-manure pile. "He should stay with his wife. Eva's had her baby now. She shouldn't have to worry about things around the house being left broken."

They dumped their loads of manure into the wagon.

It was the end of summer, and the wheat fields now lay bare and ready for fertilizing. Tata would be arriving home in two days. Elisabeth thought he would probably be very tired so she had asked Georg if he could help with this task.

Rosina, at six years old, was using a small shovel, although she wasn't terribly helpful. "Georg's head is nice," Rosina said. "So is he."

Elisabeth had to smile. Rosina had understood

Mammi's tone—she was complaining again—but not what Mammi meant.

For several years, Mammi had blamed Georg for her brother's death in the war. She had forgiven him earlier this year and now allowed him to come several days a week to help Luki learn what a man did for his family.

Like repairing a fence.

Why can't I learn how to fix a fence? Elisabeth wondered. *I already know how to paint the house, and I pound meat for schnitzel. Is using a hammer that different?*

Luki shovelled so fast that he dropped a good amount of manure onto the ground.

"Luki," Mammi scolded. "*Everything* must go into the wagon, or you can pick it up with your bare hands."

Luki froze for a moment then stared at the large mess.

"I can help." Quickly, Elisabeth began scooping up the dropped compost and manure in the hopes Mammi wouldn't have time to object.

Georg had said he would come in about an hour, but Elisabeth wondered if she'd last much longer: her shoulders were already sore.

"This stinks!" Rosina said, her small shovel in hand.

"You'll get used to it," Elisabeth said.

Luki pushed out his chest. "I'm used to it." But he wrinkled his nose.

"I should be studying," Anna added. "I want to learn more about math."

Mammi glared at her. "The only reason you're attending school is because the church will charge us if I don't send you. You're more useful here. The only math you need is to count money, and I could've taught you that myself."

Tata had taught Elisabeth that she should never stop learning. He had ensured she could read more than what she'd learned at school, that she felt comfortable turning to Luther's writings—which had been written a long time ago and therefore sometimes used different words—and that she could find her own way through the Bible. He'd also taught her about where her ancestors had come from in Germany. (Although the encyclopedia referred to it as the Holy Roman Empire. Neither she nor Tata really understood why.)

Elisabeth couldn't wait for Tata to return so they could continue their evening ritual of reading from the encyclopedia and the Bible again. Since he'd left, Mammi had given Elisabeth the responsibility of running the household, leaving her very little time to read.

Only two more days and things would truly return to normal.

"A little water for everyone?" Elisabeth asked.

When all but Mammi agreed, Elisabeth enlisted Anna's help to fetch water from the well and to carry out cups for drinking. After a short break, the shovelling continued.

Georg arrived on time, his silent manner punctuating a fight that had broken out among the younger siblings.

"Luki," he said. "A man is nice to the women around him."

"They're girls, and I'm a boy."

"I'm a *großmädchen*, Luki," Elisabeth said, referring to her new status after she'd passed her confirmation back in the spring. "I'm old enough to marry now. Only Anna and Rosina are really girls."

"Besides," Anna said, "we have to be nice to everyone. Jesus said so." She stuck out her tongue at Luki and ran off, Luki chasing after her.

Mammi threw her hands up in the air.

"I'll make sure he works harder tomorrow, when we finish repairing the ladder to the attic," Georg said.

Did the corner of Mammi's mouth curl up ever so slightly? *No. I must be dreaming*, Elisabeth thought. Mammi always said smiling made you look stupid.

"And both of those two will make sure the pig pen is so clean," Mammi said, "that Jesus Himself could visit."

Elisabeth tried not to laugh. Mammi had meant that seriously. But in her stern way, Mammi also had a sense of humour.

"What about me?" Rosina looked shaken, scared at what punishment would be doled out to her.

"You can help me in the garden."

When Rosina's eyes opened wide, Elisabeth again

fought to control a smile. Mammi wasn't punishing Rosina, but she'd make her work in a way Elisabeth couldn't.

Georg offered to take over Mammi's position to finish up the shovelling so that she and Rosina could bring their horse and its harness out of the stable.

"Stefan will meet us there?" Elisabeth's insides felt warm as she said his name.

Georg nodded, a gentle smile relaxing his otherwise habitually saddened features. "He asked me the same question about you."

Elisabeth couldn't wait to introduce Stefan formally to Tata. She had already met his family, and they'd been very nice to her. Now that Elisabeth was confirmed, she was old enough to marry. Mammi and Omama had tried to interest her in other men, like Hagel Konrad and Kaiser Michael, but Elisabeth felt Stefan respected her. Would Tata agree to let her marry him? He was the only important family member on her side left that Stefan had to meet.

When Elisabeth had first met Stefan last winter after he'd returned from the prisoner-of-war camp in Siberia, she'd embarrassed herself by staring at him and his missing arm. Then Rosina had made things worse when she loudly asked if his arm would grow back. But Stefan had taken it all in stride.

After Mammi and Rosina brought the horse and harness, Georg helped hitch up the horse, and not much longer after that, he and Elisabeth were off, with Elisabeth at the reins, something girls didn't typically do. But she wasn't thinking much about that.

Stefan was looking forward to seeing her? Or was he asking because he *didn't* want to spend time with her? But no...he wouldn't have dropped by their home last week if he didn't want to be around her.

Elisabeth's insides fluttered.

Georg laughed softly. "Your cheeks are bright red."

Elisabeth would've tried to cover them up with her hands, but she had to control the reins. She needed to change the topic. "How is Little Konrad?"

"He's doing so well. Eva and I are very blessed."

"I'm so glad to hear it. Truly, Georg."

After a pause, Georg said, "Please don't pass on what I'm about to say." Elisabeth promised she wouldn't. "We would've asked you to be his godmother—what you have done for me and Eva, despite your young age, I don't think God Himself would have words for it. But because you haven't married yet, we couldn't."

The *clip-clop* of the horse's hooves sounded just as loud to Elisabeth as her heart. "Georg...that would have been an honour. Thank you. I understand. But I don't have to be his godmother to help in any way I can."

Georg nodded and looked ahead again.

Godparents not only helped raise their godchild according to the wishes of God. They also promised to look after the child should something happen to both parents.

Since Elisabeth wasn't married, she couldn't step into that role.

It took almost an hour to reach the *salasch*, the house and farmland a few kilometres outside the village. Many German families in Semlak had such a property. Because it was customary for a father to split his land among his sons, Tata and Konrad-Bátschi had each received a portion. However, for reasons Elisabeth had never understood, Tata had received a much smaller one, while Konrad-Bátschi had been given both more land and the house. Samuel—Georg's brother—and his wife, Deaf Lissi, lived there now.

Deaf Lissi wasn't deaf but had inherited a nickname that had been passed down through several generations, as was common in Semlak. Because babies were named after family members and close friends, many people shared the same name. Elisabeth, Mammi, and Deaf Lissi were all, actually, Elisabeth Schuhmacher. Nicknames helped avoid confusion, hence Lissika, Lissa, and Deaf Lissi.

Elisabeth turned the horse onto the property. Georg jumped down and grabbed the reins to steady the horse while Elisabeth climbed down. She knocked on the dwelling's door.

Deaf Lissi was expecting her first child. So far as Elisabeth knew—because one never discussed such things—everything was going well. What Elisabeth didn't know, of course, was when God would bring the child into this world. She had read in the encyclopedia that a woman carried a baby for nine months. Elisabeth had noticed Deaf Lissi growing larger in the middle last month. She counted nine months from then. *So, the baby will be born in the new year*, she thought.

Deaf Lissi and Samuel opened the door and greeted Elisabeth with open arms. Unlike Konrad-Bátschi and Margarethe-Néni, Samuel and Deaf Lissi were kind and welcomed Elisabeth every time she came out to tend to her father's property. Georg and Stefan helped, too. In fact, Georg had offered Mammi his family's assistance in tending to the land while Tata was in America. Although Stefan wasn't part of Georg's family, their friendship was so special that it seemed that way.

But did that mean that after Tata returned home on Wednesday, Elisabeth wouldn't see Stefan as often?

"Where is Stefan?" she asked.

"Coming!" she heard him call from the side of the house. "I was just feeding the horses."

Elisabeth suddenly lost her voice.

How could this happen? All these months, she'd been able to speak to him with ease. Despite his being seven years older, he felt like a good friend to her. She had been able to trust him with some of her deepest worries.

Now, she seemed to be at a loss for words whenever she saw him. Was it because they both felt that marriage was in their future? *Did Jesus ever experience these feelings?* she wondered. She shook the thoughts out of her head. She couldn't recall any stories in the Bible about Jesus liking or marrying a woman.

Elisabeth heard Georg chuckle. She gave him a stern look. Her cousin, who was twice her age, clearly understood her. Unfortunately, her reaction made him chuckle even more.

"Let's load the shovels," Elisabeth said. She might not be able to speak directly to Stefan, but she could take charge of farm chores. Loading the shovels and rakes onto the wagon's bench helped Elisabeth feel like herself again.

Georg and Stefan led the horse to the field that had been freshly plowed, while Samuel and Elisabeth followed. Deaf Lissi stayed inside to begin canning.

Georg jumped onto the bench in the wagon and then helped up Samuel, whose one leg had been made lame from polio. The two began shovelling compost onto the ground, where Elisabeth and Stefan used rakes to spread it.

"Are you excited about your father returning?" Stefan asked.

Elisabeth pushed the compost-and-manure mixture over the ground. She could talk about her father. "I can hardly wait, but I'm so nervous that something will happen to him before he arrives home. His journey is so long."

Stefan had tucked the rake's handle under his right arm as he pulled and pushed the rake with his left hand. "I've been praying for him since you told us in June that he'd be returning." He smiled at her. "I'm looking forward to meeting him."

A shiver of excitement travelled through Elisabeth.

Samuel threw a pile of manure and compost onto the ground with his shovel. "You've never met Lukas-Bátschi?"

"Briefly, now and then, at church or in town, like any other German Semlaker. But I left for war in 1917 and only returned last winter, when he was already in America. We've never *properly* met."

Elisabeth shivered again at the implications of what the word *properly* meant.

Once they'd completed two lengths of the field, Deaf Lissi invited everyone in for lunch. Elisabeth helped her pull out the bread, smoked meat, butter, and dishes while the men sat down at the table in the front room.

When Deaf Lissi carried items to the front room, Stefan joined Elisabeth briefly in the kitchen. He picked up a plate in his hand, leaned over to her, and said in a low voice, "I have to admit, I'm nervous about meeting your father...in this way."

She understood what he was saying. Her father had the last say on whether they could marry.

"I'll do my best to say only good things about you."

Stefan's eyes filled with mischief. "You'll do your best? Will it be that difficult?"

Elisabeth face heated up. She laughed as she stared at her feet. That had not come out the way she'd wanted!

When she picked up the large platter with the food and faced the front room, everyone there was smiling at the two of them.

How could Tata refuse her desire to marry Stefan when the entire family supported them?

ELISABETH COULDN'T SLOW down the pounding of her heart. Maier Josef had been gone for several hours. Why was this last step in her father's journey taking so long? Was Tata's train late? Had he *died* on the way home?

"Lissika," Mammi said, "go inside and keep cleaning. I saw some dirt on the oven."

Elisabeth sighed but did as she was told. Once in the kitchen, she inspected the lime-covered brick oven. "I don't see..." Then she did: the tiniest smudge of soot so near to the dirt floor, it looked like the dirt floor. Elisabeth rolled her eyes, grabbed a cloth, dampened it with water from the porcelain basin on the table near the door, and cleaned up the stain. She folded the damp cloth and placed it by the basin to dry.

Men mended fences, built tools, made shoes, hammered metal in a forge, slaughtered animals for food, carved beautiful designs into wooden furniture. Their work could often be seen from afar.

What did women get to do? Clean a speck of dirt you had to bend down to see.

"Anything else I should do that no one will notice?"

But before she could answer her own question, the sound of trotting hooves from the street outside made her jump. She slipped into her shoes and ran out the door.

"Elisabeth Schuhmacher!" Mammi yelled. "A woman does not run!"

But Elisabeth didn't care. Being the tallest of the four siblings, she passed them all, almost hitting Rosina with the first gate as she whipped it open.

Slowly climbing down from the wagon was a man in strange blue pants, a cotton shirt, black vest, and a black hat.

Elisabeth didn't recognize the clothing, but she knew Tata. He had barely stepped down from the bench when Elisabeth threw herself at him, knocking him against the wagon.

Tears streamed down her face as she pushed it into his shoulder and pulled him as close as she could. A few moments later, she felt the impact of her siblings as they joined in.

Elisabeth's overwhelming happiness and relief caught in her throat: she couldn't say a word.

Tata's voice touched her ears: "I'm so glad to see you, too, Lissika."

Elisabeth pulled him in even tighter.

CHAPTER FIVE

The class questionnaire asked Juliana to list five interests.

And only five.

She began with a separate list to collect all her interests, and then she would pick the best five. That seemed like a good idea.

- tap (love it)
- jazz (like it)
- ballet (kind of like it)
- talking to my friends
- learning about my great-grandmother
- figuring out Elisabeth's book
- talking to my Opa

- eating with Sophie at Casimiro's
- reading
- studying (okay, sort of, but I like learning)
- practising
- performing for others
- talking with my parents (which is weird, but it kind of happened since we've been here)
- listening to Uncle Peter's jokes (also weird—he's funny/not funny...in a funny way)

"How am I supposed to choose only five?" Juliana asked herself.

Banging from the basement interrupted her thoughts. Opa was at it again. Juliana had tried calming him before by turning on his television. Only thirty minutes ago.

Rachel came into Juliana's room. "Your grandfather..."

His bedroom was directly under hers, so the banging was louder there.

Juliana sighed. "I was hoping to finish this list for my class." More banging. "But he needs help before he hurts himself."

Juliana got up from her desk, passed Rachel, and headed downstairs.

"Opa?"

His shirt buttons were mismatched.

"I don't know where I put it." He threw open his closet

door, but most of its contents were already on the floor. Juliana had tried helping him search for "it" yesterday—Opa wouldn't tell her what "it" was—but that had only prolonged his agony. She remembered that distraction could work with Alzheimer's patients.

"Opa, why don't we clean this up? Then it'll be easier for you to look." Okay, not much of a distraction, but at least it was something, right?

Opa shook his head. "It's maybe in the closet. Everything must stay out here." He pointed to his bed. "Or maybe it's under here." Juliana helped him lift the heavy mattress, but there was nothing.

Juliana hated seeing this side of her grandfather. She understood his reactions weren't his fault—she had learned enough about dementia over the months to know that—but he was still the only grandparent she had, and she had only really gotten to know him after her family moved here.

"How can I help?"

His eyes were wide with panic. "Isn't it clear? I need help by looking."

Since Juliana couldn't think of another option, she dug in. Rachel showed up at the bedroom door a few minutes later, an expression on her face that said she'd help. Juliana shook her head. In this state, Opa might not recognize her, and that might frighten him. Or anger him. Or...Juliana didn't know what.

After ten minutes of fruitless searching, an idea finally occurred to Juliana.

"Opa, you keep searching down here, and I'll go look upstairs, okay?"

Opa nodded as he kept throwing clothes across the room. A belt buckle hit the wall.

Upstairs, Juliana apologized to Rachel.

"Jules, I'm not going to take offense at something like that. I get it. You're in a tough spot."

Juliana pulled bread, butter, and salami out of the fridge. "Thanks. I just wish Mom and Dad would do... something. Mom mentioned an appointment with the neurologist, but this photograph issue... I'm scared I'm going to make the wrong decision and somehow hurt him more."

Rachel came up behind Juliana and laid a hand on her shoulder. "You're doing the right thing: trying to help. No one can ask any more of you."

Juliana popped the bread into the toaster and pulled out a butter knife.

"Are you hungry already? It's only nine-thirty."

"I'm hoping the smell of the salami will distract him. It's his favourite snack, and he loves the salami they sell at Mom's store. You're supposed to distract Alzheimer's patients when their brain takes over like this, instead of joining in whatever their obsession is."

Five minutes later, Juliana had two open-faced sand-wiches on a plate. "Wish me luck."

She headed downstairs and entered Opa's room. "Opa? I thought you might want something to eat."

At first, he didn't stop, and Juliana worried she'd have to call her mom—there was no way this level of stress was healthy for him.

But then he looked up. "Salami?"

"I thought you might need something to give you more energy."

Opa seemed to deliberate for a moment. "You're right. But I can't eat down here. I have to eat upstairs. We eat upstairs, Yulika. Always. Eating in your bedroom leaves crumbs, and then you get ants."

Soon the two were back in the kitchen, seated at the small round table. Rachel came in.

"Good morning, Rachel," Opa said. "It's nice to meet you!"

Juliana and Rachel exchanged glances, but Rachel had learned to roll with the punches. She smiled and extended her hand, which Opa accepted. "It's nice to meet you, too, Mr. Schuhmacher. I hear you've been looking after Juliana really well."

Opa laughed. "I think she looks more after me!" He pointed to the plate on the table. "See?"

Just like that, the happy, self-confident Opa Juliana knew had returned.

Rachel's glance at Juliana made it clear she was beginning to understand how hard it was for Juliana to live with her grandfather.

After Opa finished his snack, Juliana suggested he go for a walk. Although she worried about him going out by himself, he had returned every time other than one time when he'd had a panic attack. The only other choice she could think of was television in his messy bedroom, where he might start obsessing again over "it."

At least the weather is nice, she thought, *and the neighbours know him.*

Opa glanced out the front window. "The sun is shining. A walk is something good."

Once he was out the door, Juliana set a timer on her phone. "I'll call Mom if he doesn't come home in thirty minutes," she explained to Rachel. *Of course, if Mom would find ways to look after him, I wouldn't have to worry about him like this.*

"That's honestly the best you can do."

Juliana cleaned up the sandwich ingredients and wiped down the counter.

"Just a question," Rachel said, "but should we put his room back in order? Would that help avoid reminding him he was looking for something?"

Juliana loved the idea, and they headed downstairs immediately.

"Just avoid that bottom drawer in his chest," Juliana said.

"Why?"

Juliana laughed. "I opened it once as I was putting away his laundry and found a long braid in there. Mom told me it was my grandmother's hair. I guess she cut it off at some point in her thirties when women began to wear their hair short."

Rachel's mouth turned upside down. "Hasn't she been dead since we were little?"

"Eleven years ago."

"Thanks for the warning."

After twenty minutes, everything was back in its place and the girls were upstairs in Juliana's tiny room. She barely had space for a chair between her twin bed and desk, and her closet was perhaps only four feet wide.

Only then did Juliana have a moment to breathe. A familiar aching feeling of anxiety grew in her stomach. She took a deep breath to calm herself. After all, she didn't want to burden Rachel with her issues when Rachel was still dealing with the death of her mom. Surely, Juliana could handle Opa's behaviour, right? At least until her parents stepped in?

She pulled her knees up to her chest to ease the anxiety.

"Hey," Rachel said. "Tell me what's going on in your head."

Juliana didn't want to say anything. If she just waited another minute, the sensation would disappear. It usually did.

Rachel sighed. "I don't know why you think you can wall yourself up like this on me. I've known you for most of your life." She glanced around Juliana's room. "Ah, there it is." She reached over to the desk and picked up Elisabeth's journal. "What picture are you at?"

Juliana turned the pages to one about three-quarters through the old journal.

Rachel studied it. "A house…"

"I think it might have been Elisabeth's house, but I don't really know, and I don't want to ask Opa in case he starts getting upset about her photo again."

"Makes sense." Rachel studied it a little more. "She was our age, you said?"

Juliana nodded. "She seemed to get better with each drawing. There's a lot more shading in this one than previous ones. Look."

Juliana flipped back a little, pointed out some drawings, like the one with Georg, and the one with an overturned table and two chairs.

"There's a lot more detail too," Rachel said.

This drawing had realistic shading under parts of the thatch roof to show where the sun was shining. It also had flowers, one of those trees Juliana called an "upside down tree," where the branches grew mostly toward the ground, and what looked like two gates—one near the front of the property and one farther back. Vague shading hinted at other buildings. Some chickens pecked around in the background, too.

"What do you make of it?" Rachel asked. "Why would she draw this?"

Juliana released her knees and sat forward. "I've been wondering that, too. She drew her kitchen on the first page and what Opa called the front room on the second. That's kind of a family room and communal bedroom in one. Some of these drawings are of someone's baking—hers? her mom's? I don't know. Then there are four pairs of shoes..." Juliana turned to the part in the book with sketches of shoes with interesting designs. "I don't know what those are about. Opa couldn't remember either when I asked. He said only men were shoemakers back then. Maybe they were what Elisabeth wanted." Juliana showed Rachel the lantern, the photo with a pair of mittens being pulled off, someone's burial...

"Oh, sorry," she said as she realized the content of that drawing. She should've thought more carefully: it had only been a few months since Rachel's mother died.

Rachel sighed. "I don't need to be protected. If this drawing makes me sad, let it make me sad. If I don't react to it, let that be okay, too."

Juliana's shoulders slouched. "Sorry. Just wanted to, you know, make sure you're okay."

Rachel nodded to acknowledge she accepted the apology. "But let me help you for once instead."

"For once? Rach, don't you know how often you've helped me since I left home? You've been encouraging, supportive, and honest with me. You get me when my family doesn't. Which still happens a lot. It was really hard studying for those first exams by myself when Mom and Dad weren't around to help with Opa. And now the same thing is happening again."

"You need to talk to them."

"I tried last week, when Opa got angry because he couldn't find the salami in the fridge. And then when I was finishing getting everything ready for you Saturday, Mom said she was worried about Opa, but she only talked about his upcoming neurologist appointment. I want to help him..." Juliana clenched her jaw and let out a sharp breath. "But I'm fifteen. When Mom asked us to move back to her childhood home to look after Opa, I thought Mom and Dad would be looking after him, and I'd get to have fun with him like a granddaughter's supposed to."

Juliana opened the journal again to the drawing of what she believed to be Elisabeth's house. "I feel like I'm caught between worlds: Calgary and here. I miss my life in Calgary—you, graduating at the end of grade nine, our dance studio. But if I moved back, I'd miss Opa and Sophie and Aunt Anne and crazy Uncle Peter." She slowly paged through the journal. "I know Elisabeth eventually moved away—Opa was born in Temeswar but grew up in Semlak. Did she feel like she was torn between two worlds, too? Or her father. How did he feel when he moved back after spending a year in the States?"

"Maybe things at home changed so much that he didn't know how to adjust. I mean, look at everything that's happened to us since you moved: my mom, your dad taking a new job and driving you bananas even though you wanted him home..."

"Opa's condition worsening..." Juliana closed the book. "I mean...and please don't repeat this to Sophie...I don't get why Aunt Anne and Uncle Peter aren't stepping in either. Or even Uncle Phillip. I get that Opa's not his father...but why are the adults in my family leaving everything to me?"

Neither girl said anything for several minutes. Juliana did indeed feel like her family had just assumed she'd take care of Opa.

"What would Elisabeth have done in my situation?"

"From what you've told me, she handled everything with help from her family."

"But who?"

A noise from the kitchen told Juliana that Opa had returned home. A minute later, the muffled voices of his television show wafted through the floor. Nothing to signal that he'd resumed his searching. She turned off the timer on her phone.

"Maybe you have to ask for help," Rachel said. "From

everyone. If there's one thing I've learned, it's that parents are excellent at avoiding topics that hit too close to home."

Juliana thought for a moment, then reached for her phone and dialled. "Uncle Peter? I'm worried about Opa. Do you have time to talk?"

CHAPTER SIX

So much had happened in the past ten months: Konrad-Bátschi's death, Elisabeth's confirmation, Georg's support, Mammi's lost baby...

Not expecting all her feelings to break out of her like this, Elisabeth squeezed Tata even tighter.

When Mammi had lost her baby earlier this year, Elisabeth hadn't even known she'd been expecting. One simply didn't speak about where babies came from. To have Tata there to help Mammi would've made the loss easier for Mammi to bear. Elisabeth was certain.

From deep in his chest Elisabeth heard Tata's light chuckle. "My Lissika, I need to breathe."

She jumped back, knocking Anna to the ground.

"I'm so sorry!" She offered her sister her hand.

A scowl on her face, Anna pushed Elisabeth out of the

way and hugged their father as tightly as she could, while Luki tried to shove his arm in front of Anna. Only then did Elisabeth notice one person missing from their tiny crowd: Rosina.

The youngest Schuhmacher child instead had hidden herself in Mammi's skirt.

"Rosina?" Elisabeth called to her sister. "Come here."

Rosina shook her head as Mammi pried her loose and pushed her away, but Rosina simply grabbed Mammi's skirt in her small fists.

Mammi tried to walk toward her husband, but Rosina kept pulling her back. Wanting to let her mother and father meet again, Elisabeth softly removed her sister's hand from Mammi's skirt.

Sadness clouded Tata's face. "Rosina doesn't recognize me," he said. "Just like after the war."

Tata had gone to war when Rosina was two, returned after two years, and then left a year and a half later for America. During the years when Rosina would've gotten to know her father, he'd been absent.

"Let me talk to her," Elisabeth said.

Tata reached out to Mammi and pulled her hands to his heart. They touched foreheads. Mammi's body shuddered gently. Elisabeth believed she was crying, though Mammi would, of course, never show tears to her children.

Elisabeth beckoned her other siblings to join them,

partly to help Rosina recognize her father, and partly to give Mammi and Tata a little time without prying eyes.

She crouched down to Rosina's level. "Do you know who that is?"

The little girl shook her head.

"That's Tata," Anna said.

"Tata...?"

Luki crossed his arms. "I know who he is."

Elisabeth squeezed Luki's elbow to signal to him to be quiet. She returned her attention to Rosina. "Do you remember that he went to America to bring back money for us? And that we've been talking about how excited we all are that he's coming back home?"

Anna touched her younger sister's arm. "For a new roof."

Rosina was still confused. An idea flew into Elisabeth's mind. "You should show Tata the scarf you've been knitting for him."

"Knitting?" She stared at her father again. "Tata! I'm making you a scarf!" Rosina ran to her father and almost knocked him and Mammi over.

Mammi wiped her eyes before turning around to face her children, but her eyes looked a little red.

Tata kneeled down, smiled, and hugged Rosina, tears welling in his eyes, too. "I should never have left. I missed my family so much."

"Come inside, Lukas," Mammi said to her husband.

"The girls will bring out some food, and Luki wants to tell you about everything he's learned from..." She sighed. "From Georg."

Meier Josef and Tata carried Tata's luggage into the house as the girls pulled out food.

With Tata now returned, Elisabeth couldn't wait to sit down with him in the evening to read more from the encyclopedia and Martin Luther's teachings. Just as she had been learning about the war from Stefan, now Tata could teach her about life in America.

Most importantly, Elisabeth couldn't help but wonder when she should talk to Tata about Stefan.

THE CHILDREN and Mammi stayed out of the front room for several hours while Tata refreshed himself and slept. At the supper table, he said very little. This was unlike Tata before he'd left, when he would talk about the village, the news... anything to teach his children more about the world.

Elisabeth was eager to learn about the clothing he had worn, but she prayed to Jesus for patience. *He's probably too tired from the journey*, she thought. After spending more than two weeks travelling—a train from Harrisburg to New York City, then a boat to Germany, followed by different trains to Romania, and ending with the wagon ride with Meier Josef—Tata must be exhausted.

But Elisabeth and her siblings chattered away, with Mammi correcting them as usual.

Only after supper was cleared did Tata speak. "It's so good to eat food my family has made. And to sleep on a straw bed." He folded his hands in his lap. "It was a mistake to have left. Had I known that so much would happen while I was away, I would've stayed."

Mammi's face relaxed. "Lukas, you brought home enough money for a new roof. That already is a lot."

All the children's eyes opened wide. "Really?" Elisabeth said. "That much?"

Tata sighed as he nodded. "But to not be here for my brother's passing and your..." He glanced cautiously at Mammi. "Your illness...I would gladly give up that money to have been here."

Part of Elisabeth boiled at the thought of giving up all that money for a man as mean as Konrad-Bátschi. She recalled how her uncle had left Georg covered in gravel in the centre of the village, his mind full of fearful memories and dreams from that war. Her memory of Georg's face when he'd realized that his father had abandoned him would never leave Elisabeth. That wasn't the love of a father.

Another part of her admonished her for thinking like that: family had to stay together, no matter what.

But to have Tata home to help Mammi when she lost the baby would have been a blessing.

"And I don't have enough to marry off Elisabeth. Rent and other expenses were much more than I thought they would be. I needed at least another six months."

Tata was thinking about her marriage. Elisabeth's heart beat the way it did when she saw Stefan.

Mammi nodded solemnly. "I can continue with my shoe designs. They've become very popular."

To Elisabeth's surprise, Tata shook his head. "I will not have my wife working for money. What would that say about me? Besides, I would rather enjoy your wonderful cooking and baking again. I need to teach Luki the trade. There isn't enough room in the workshop for all of us."

"I can move to the front room, where you used to work," Mammi said. "The embroidery doesn't cause a smell, and there's little to clean up when I finish."

Tata shook his head again. "That will make me look like a failure, Lissa. Everyone will think I left my family alone to bring back more money and failed. No."

A flash of disappointment appeared on Mammi's face, and Elisabeth felt pity for her. In her eyes, Mammi had become proud of her work and the chance to earn money. But she would not argue with her husband about this. Keeping the kitchen clean, yes. But earning her own money? Never.

Unless...

"I can help Mammi," Elisabeth said. "It'll improve my embroidery, too."

Tata began shaking his head before Elisabeth could even finish. "After you told me about how Anna was treated by other children," he said, "I realized that my leaving hurt my family in more ways than I could have guessed. We don't need more gossip that might also affect your chances of marrying well."

Elisabeth left the topic alone. Obviously, now was not a good time to tell Tata who she wanted to marry. If she prayed to Jesus, would He help her find a good time?

As Mammi and the girls cleared away the supper dishes, Elisabeth asked Tata the question she'd been burning to ask for weeks: "Can you teach me again from the encyclopedia set? There were so many things I didn't understand by myself."

Tata brushed crumbs off his lap. "Too much has changed, Lissika. The future of shoemaking is uncertain. Luki needs to learn the trade *and* be good in school work so he can support his own family, and all of you, in case something happens to me...like it happened to my brother."

The mood in the room became sombre.

"Let's not think like that," Mammi said. "You've just come home." She walked into the back room, pulled down a bottle of schnapps, and poured some into a very small glass for Tata.

"But we must," he said. "We also have to make sure our girls marry men who can take care of them. Farmers will never lose their jobs. I don't think a mill operator will either. And with all the technology I saw in America... Lissa, I had electricity in my house. It often went out, and I missed the warmth of our gas lamps, but to touch something on the wall and turn on a light... The world is changing quickly. We have to prepare for that."

Mammi shook her head. "Why fix what isn't broken? Our gas lamps work just fine."

"Maybe so. But I think a man who knows how to work with machines is a good idea. I don't think that even a blacksmith will have much of a future."

"How could all these people be put out of work?"

Tata took a sip of his schnapps. "Factories make work, but they mean moving to the city. Factories also make goods cheaper. Shoes are cheaper in America because of their shoe factories."

"But that is America."

"It will come here. Make no mistake. We already use factories to make fabric—do you remember in our childhood how our mothers and grandmothers harvested flax, turned it into thread, and wove fabric?" Mammi nodded. "Is it not easier to sew clothing without having to make fabric first?" Mammi nodded again. "Luki can't rely on making shoes to support his family, and we must be careful how the men who are to marry our daughters make their living."

Could Stefan work with machines? Elisabeth had never

thought of that. If he couldn't, would Tata refuse to allow Elisabeth and Stefan to marry?

Tata ran his hand over his head. "America has many factories that made weapons for the war. The war is over, so they need something else to make. Don't forget that I worked in a cigar factory. They have factories for almost everything now."

The atmosphere at the table felt like church on Good Friday—solemn and sad—only here without the hope of resurrection.

Tata continued. "I repaired shoes for some in the neighbourhood, but I also met two shoemakers from Italy who said they closed their shops and worked in factories because their shops were losing money. The factories were making money." He drank the last of his schnapps and passed the glass to Elisabeth to wash. "Come, Luki. Let Mammi and your sisters clean up. You have to study. A lot is going to change here."

As Elisabeth, Anna, and Rosina helped Mammi wash the dishes, Tata and Luki remained in the front room, an encyclopedia open on the table.

The change in Tata hurt Elisabeth's heart. Had life in America been so difficult? Why had he not said anything? *Probably so we wouldn't worry about him*, she thought. Should she have shared so many sad details with him in her letters? But if she hadn't—and if Georg hadn't sent that telegram to inform Tata of Mammi's condition—then he would still be in America.

She glanced up at the cross hanging above the door to the front room. *You travelled a lot, didn't You? When You were twelve and celebrating Passover in Jerusalem, You stayed behind to learn from the priests. You also preached in many different places. Did You change? Did You miss Your home? Your parents?*

As always, Jesus didn't answer her.

After she finished her chores, she returned to drawing. Tata's trunk was still open in the back room, airing out, and she would begin washing his clothes tomorrow. If her book was to show everything important that had happened while Tata had been gone, then she needed to draw the trunk. She hung some of his clothes over its edges to show what had been inside.

Book and pencil in hand, she began drawing.

CHAPTER SEVEN

Juliana, Rachel, and Sophie dropped into comfy beanbag chairs in the reading nook in Sophie's house, each holding two photo albums from Aunt Anne's collection. If they were going to find a replacement photo for Opa, this was the easiest place to start, because the photos were somewhat organized. Uncle Peter would join them in an hour with Opa's photos after Opa left the house to spend time with his friends. They didn't want Opa to know about the search, worried that Opa would fall into another panic attack.

Juliana had brought Elisabeth's journal of drawings, and now she opened it to several pages that had faces on them. The three girls took photos with their phone so they had a hint of who they might be looking for.

"Sophie?" Aunt Anne called to her daughter from the kitchen.

Sophie heaved a heavy sigh and went to see what her mom wanted.

Aunt Anne spoke to her daughter in a low voice, but Juliana and Rachel could hear Sophie answer with a curt "No."

Juliana pointed to her eyes. "Probably about her glasses," she whispered.

Sophie had a special pair of glasses with telescopic lenses attached—something like what a surgeon might wear during an operation. They made seeing immensely easier, but they also embarrassed her. She had begun wearing them in front of Juliana recently, which Juliana took as a huge sign of trust. Unfortunately, Sophie's older sister Rebecca regularly badgered Sophie to wear them to the point that it had become a sore spot. Sophie also didn't wear the glasses at school, and she was already bullied enough for her eyesight.

The girls could hear Aunt Anne sigh as Sophie rejoined them in the reading nook. Juliana wished she could have something like it: two walls of books, three brightly coloured beanbag chairs on the floor, and a matching couch against the third wall, with windows above it. The reading nook seemed to say, "Forget the world and lose yourself in a book." As much as Juliana loved to lose herself in dance, that wasn't possible late at night when people were sleeping or if she herself was totally exhausted. Reading came in at a close second to dancing.

The girls decided to ignore the albums with colour photos—they were too recent. Juliana put the albums they didn't need back onto their shelves and pulled out others with black-and-white and sepia photos.

"What about this one?" Rachel asked after about ten minutes. She held up a black-and-white photo of a middle-aged woman wearing pants, her hair styled in a beehive, standing in the downtown of a city. Elisabeth had moved to a city in Romania called Temeswar at some point. Maybe this was it?

"Elisabeth died in the '60s," Juliana said, "so the hairstyle fits. Aunt Anne?"

Aunt Anne came into the room, inspected the photo and shook her head. "I don't know who this is, but I think she's too young. And Elisabeth never came to Canada. This is downtown Kitchener. You probably didn't recognize it because so much has changed."

Everyone had a good chuckle at the mistake, and Juliana took a picture of the photo. "So we can identify downtown Kitchener again if we need to."

"Good thinking," Sophie said.

They continued searching, sometimes asking Aunt Anne for her opinion, each time learning a clue that showed them the photo wasn't the right one.

"How's your career project coming along?" Rachel

asked. "You've barely worked on it. Isn't your report due Monday?"

Juliana continued flipping through album pages. "I did what I needed to for my course today. The rest can wait a little—I want to spend time with both of you!"

Sophie knit her eyebrows together. "Wait...you're ignoring school? Is everything okay?"

Rachel laughed until she realized it was a serious question. "Sorry."

"It's just not like Juliana," Sophie said.

Juliana slouched back into her beanbag. "I just don't know where to start."

"I get it," Rachel said. "You want to do it perfectly, so you haven't started at all."

"That makes sense," Sophie said. "You always do things a hundred and ten percent."

Juliana hated it when someone knew her so well they could call her out on something. And now she had two such people in front of her. "Maybe I shouldn't have introduced you to one another." She smiled. "It was easier to defend myself against each of you alone."

Rachel flipped a page. "You divided and conquered with us, is that it?"

"We were already divided," Sophie said, with a smile. "She just had to conquer."

"Good point."

Juliana rolled her eyes.

"But still," Rachel said. "You need to figure this out, Jules. You'll never write a thousand words in a weekend."

"Up to a thousand," Juliana corrected. "We can hand in seven hundred and fifty."

Rachel put down the book she had in her hand. "And you're going to do the minimum?"

Juliana's cheeks heated up. Of course, Rachel knew Juliana's gold standard. Why demonstrate your abilities in seven hundred and fifty words when you had an extra two hundred and fifty to show more?

"You know me too well. Do you need a new album to search?" Her report was off-limits the rest of the afternoon as far as she was concerned.

As they searched through the photos, Juliana saw that Rachel kept taking quick glances at Sophie, as though she wanted to ask something but was holding herself back.

Please don't ask about her glasses, Juliana thought. *She'll stop wearing them in front of me, too.* She hadn't thought to caution Rachel before they'd arrived.

A photo album slipped out of Sophie's hands as she tried to hold it closer to her eyes. These albums were heavy.

"I promise I won't laugh at your glasses," Rachel said. "If they make it easier for you, you know, to…"

She stopped when Sophie took in an angry breath and didn't say anything.

How could Juliana tell her best friend to drop it without

giving Sophie the impression she couldn't speak up for herself?

Rachel continued, her voice cautious. "I mean...I know what it's like to have some kind of invisible mark on you that everyone else sees and so they treat you differently."

"That's right. *Invisible*. My glasses are *obvious*."

Rachel hung her head. "I'm sorry. I'm not saying this well at all." She took another deep breath. "Everyone at home treats me differently because I lost my mom. They expect me to be happy when I'm sad, sad when I'm happy... it's hard. I just wanted to tell you that you can be yourself in front of me."

Sophie looked up, the expression on her face softer. "Oh." She swallowed. "I didn't mean to get angry about that."

"You don't have to apologize." Rachel tugged at a loose thread on her shorts. "I'm not saying this in the best way. I...I just don't want you to feel you have to hide yourself in front of me. I have to do that at school and at dance... I don't like it."

Juliana's heart grew ten times bigger, and then sank to her feet: she hadn't realized Rachel felt that way. But she was filled with joy to see that Rachel felt so comfortable sharing openly with Sophie, someone she had just met a few days before, and that Sophie seemed to be warming up to Rachel. She had known the two would get along, but this was more than she had hoped for.

Sophie stood up, still looking a bit unsure. "Okay," she said slowly. As Sophie headed upstairs, Juliana caught Aunt Anne's mouth wide open. Juliana had to smile in spite of herself. Friendships—even new ones—could move mountains.

A few minutes later, Sophie returned with her glasses. "Here they are."

"How do they work?" Rachel asked.

"They make things a lot bigger. So I can see faces and stuff like that. And read regular things, so long as the print isn't too small."

Rachel's smile was gentle. "Sounds awesome."

"Except they make me look stupid." But despite her comment, Sophie cautiously put on her glasses. The telescopic lenses in the middle made her irises and pupils look large. Juliana understood Sophie's embarrassment around them—there was nothing worse for a teen than being different from everyone else. *Except the popular kids*, Juliana thought. *They can be different. Dress how they want. Style their hair how they want.*

Teen life was sometimes truly unfair.

Sophie picked up a photo album. Juliana and Rachel followed suit. But after another hour of fruitless searching, they sighed in collective surrender.

Sophie removed her glasses, rubbed her eyes, and set the glasses on a nearby end table. Then she turned to Juliana.

"I don't get it. You're having a hard time starting your career project, and yet we just spent...I don't know...at least an hour? More? Looking at photos."

"I'm telling you," Rachel said. "Perfectionism at its finest."

Juliana crossed her arms. "We're starting with that again?"

Sophie shook her head. "We're continuing with it. You need to get started."

"Have you seen her in a last-minute panic?" Rachel asked.

Sophie pointed to her glasses. "I put those on. You can start your project."

Her comment hit home. Juliana understood how much trust it took Sophie to wear those in front of them. Maybe it was time she opened up to them, too.

"It's more than that. It's that I'm terrified I'm going to discover there's no room in my life for dance." She stared at the closed photo album on her lap. "What if my career comes with such a demand on my time—like lots and lots of studying or a lot of hours at work or being away from home for weeks on end—and there's no room for dance?"

"Like your dad?" Rachel asked.

"And Uncle Peter?" Sophie added.

Juliana nodded. "How can I dance if I'm gone all the time?"

Sophie shrugged. "Find another job?"

"I suppose. But all I ever hear is 'you'll never have a forty-hour work week.' I mean, look at my mom: if she's not at work, she's answering texts, sometimes phone calls. There's no way she'd have time to dance."

Sophie nodded thoughtfully. "And Mr. Casimiro is always at the restaurant."

"Right?"

"And Miss Kasia is always at the studio." Rachel was referring to Juliana's former dance teacher in Calgary. "She takes one night a week off, but she's otherwise there. Then there's competition." Rachel counted quietly to herself. "She'll easily do fifty hours in four days of comp. Maybe even sixty."

"Exactly. They all do what they love—or at least enjoy —and it's more than forty hours a week. What if I'm too tired at the end of work to dance?"

Just then, the doorbell rang. A minute later, Uncle Peter with his mullet and telltale grin showed up, a wooden desk drawer of photos in his hands and plastic bags filled with more photos hanging from his wrists.

Juliana appreciated the interruption.

"I didn't want to damage the photos," he said, "so, I just brought the drawer."

"Rachel, this is Uncle Peter." Juliana winked at her uncle. "For better or worse."

Uncle Peter feigned a dramatic gasp. "That's not how you speak to your elders."

"I treat my elders with respect, Uncle Peter," Rachel said, laughing. Then she clapped her hand over her mouth. "Can I call you Uncle Peter? Juliana does. Obviously. And you look like an uncle type."

Uncle Peter laughed out loud. "I'll ask you later what an 'uncle type' looks like." He set the drawer and shopping bags down. "But I always have room for another niece or nephew."

Juliana wished her family would adopt Rachel: she'd fit right in.

Uncle Peter groaned as he got down on the floor. As he opened the bags, he asked how the search was going. Juliana filled him in on their progress. Sophie put her glasses back on, and everyone dug in. Within a half hour, the girls and Uncle Peter only had a few small piles of black-and-white and sepia photos left to look at.

"Wow," Juliana said. "Those are so cool." She lifted one up. "I still can't believe women dressed like this."

The photo showed two women, each with her hair covered by a kerchief. On their upper bodies, they wore what looked like a black blazer or jacket—it had long sleeves, seemed to fit the torso well, and finished with a bit of fabric that fanned out at the bottom and over the skirt. The skirt itself flowed almost to the ankles and looked quite full.

"I can't imagine 'dressing up' like that," Rachel said.

"Ugh, me neither," Sophie replied. "How do you move?"

Uncle Peter laughed. "From what I saw at the German club when I was a kid, and many of the women still wore skirts like that...you'd be surprised how well they moved when they danced a polka or a waltz. Quite stunning."

"But does this mean this is from Semlak?" Juliana asked.

Uncle Peter nodded. "Let's start a specific album for Semlak photos. The oils on our skin can damage them over time if we touch them too often."

Aunt Anne joined the group, and they eventually collected all the photos from Semlak—including some from Aunt Anne's collections—into one album.

"Change of topic," Uncle Peter said as he began comparing the people in the photos to drawings in Elisabeth's book. "First, thank you both for looking after Tata yesterday morning. None of us knew about the picture in his pocket."

"No idea at all," Aunt Anne confirmed.

"Your mom told me the two of you cleaned his room," Uncle Peter said.

Juliana and Rachel nodded. "It only took us maybe twenty minutes or so, but we thought it might distract him from looking for whatever it was he wanted. But now that I think about it...was that lying to him?"

Uncle Peter and Aunt Anne shook their heads, and Aunt Anne explained: "Lying to cover your tracks is one thing. But with someone in Tata's condition, hiding something extremely upsetting from them—that's okay. We know we're trying to make him feel better."

Juliana took what her aunt said to heart. "I'm worried I'm going to do something that'll hurt him."

Uncle Peter set the album he was working on aside. "That's too much weight for a fifteen-year-old to carry. I'm glad you called me."

"Juliana," Aunt Anne said, "*never* think that what you're doing is the wrong thing. You just handle the situation as best as you can. If anything, I'm embarrassed I wasn't there to help."

"Your mom said the same thing," Uncle Peter said. "All three of us discussed it, and we're going to look at getting a PSW for him."

Aunt Anne breathed in deeply. "It's time."

"A what?" Sophie asked.

"Personal support worker," Uncle Peter answered. "Someone who helps with daily chores and tasks but also looks after the person while they're there. Katy thinks she can adjust her work hours a little to help more, but Paul's hours are pretty fixed. If we can find someone Tata trusts, then they can take him out for walks, maybe even to the club. And they can suggest activities to keep him busy so he's not just watching TV downstairs. Annie and I will help more, too, where we can."

Juliana felt relief that the family was taking steps to help Opa.

But she also felt despair at their search: although they got a sense of the clothes and backgrounds from thatched roofs on to men's pants that almost looked like baggy jodhpurs, no one had found any image of anyone who could be Elisabeth Schuhmacher.

Suddenly she shot her hands in the air. "Oh my god, I've got it! When Opa said he was looking for 'it,' I thought he meant the photo that got destroyed in the wash. But he didn't!"

"What else could he have meant?" Rachel asked.

"There's another photo! In his room!"

Everyone stopped.

Juliana continued. "He said things like, 'It must be in the closet' and 'It must be under my bed.' I know he's forgetting things, and I know that Alzheimer's sometimes makes people not make sense. But I think he knew there was another photo."

Uncle Peter looked at his watch. "Katy will be bringing him home in about thirty minutes. I'll call her and ask her to delay him," he said.

Juliana kicked her feet in the air. "I'm finally going to see Elisabeth!"

CHAPTER EIGHT

*E*lisabeth thanked the shopkeeper for the bag of beet sugar, and she and Maria began walking home, the gravel street crunching under their ankle-high leather boots.

"You must be excited to show your father how well you bake now."

Friends and family had been invited to stop by the Schuhmacher home on Sunday afternoon to celebrate Tata's safe arrival back to Semlak. Elisabeth only had three days to prepare, and Saturday would already be dedicated to giving the house a thorough cleaning. Mammi was very busy finishing her last shoe orders.

Maria's eyes lit up in anticipation. "I certainly can't wait for Sunday so I can have some of your rum roll. Oh! Can I help you make it? Konrad wants me to bake better before we marry. And I only have five months left."

A rum roll was perhaps the hardest item to bake. The cake was first baked at maybe one thumb-width high on a flat tray. It was then rolled to cool, unrolled to fill, and rolled again to finish. Any mistake at any of those stages and the cake would rip. Buttercream filling could cover up small tears in the cake, but a full tear would embarrass not only Elisabeth but also Mammi.

However, it was also Tata's favourite cake, one he'd said a few times he had sorely missed.

Elisabeth quickly agreed to Maria's request to teach her how to bake better. But she wasn't keen on Maria's engagement with Hagel Konrad. He had proposed marriage to Elisabeth, and she had flatly refused him. He was condescending, rude, and—to be honest—stupid. But he met the requirements of a "good husband": he was a carpenter, he would inherit his father's land, and he earned well because of his skills. Elisabeth understood that. But her own requirements were higher: Elisabeth needed someone who would treat her as his equal. Any man she married would have to allow her to talk about the war and things that happened in the world, which the war had made bigger to her. She would want him to ask for her opinion on these matters and allow her to leave Thursday mornings for the weekly news and mail.

Someone like Stefan.

Elisabeth did not want to end up like her mother, who, despite usually barking orders around the household and cutting people down with her words, obeyed Tata the moment he said she was not to work anymore.

If I want to work to earn money, my husband must let me, she thought. In her own, silent way, Mammi had found pride in offering something no one else in Semlak could. Why should Tata take that away from her?

"You seem quiet," Maria said.

"Just thinking about my future husband."

Maria giggled and poked her. "Here he comes."

Elisabeth's cheeks turned hotter than the bright sunshine in August as Stefan and Georg walked in their direction.

Stefan doffed his cap and Georg nodded.

"A beautiful day, isn't it?" Stefan said.

"The sun is bright." Georg smiled.

But why was everyone acting so strangely around her and Stefan? Elisabeth had thought she was the only one who was behaving so oddly around Stefan. Clearly, though, everyone else was, too.

"It's very bright," Elisabeth answered. "But very hot!"

Stefan removed his cap, revealing his short, clean haircut. He fanned his face quickly. "A day for work in the shade if possible." He put his cap back on.

Did Stefan hold eye contact with her a little longer than

usual? *No*, Elisabeth thought. *It's just the glare of the sun lighting up his eyes.*

Then she remembered what he'd said just a few days ago, on Monday: "I'm nervous about meeting your father... in this way."

He *did* like her. Or at least, he wanted to marry her.

I have no land, hardly a dowry worth mentioning, and otherwise no important possessions, Elisabeth thought. *So he doesn't want to marry me for the property I would come with. Why, then?*

Elisabeth changed the subject to ease this uncomfortable tension that had come out of nowhere. "What are you doing today, Stefan?"

He looked at the bag of sugar in her hand. "Probably the same as you. Buying a few items Georg needs for his workshop, and..." Now his cheeks turned red. "I was hoping I'd run into you."

Elisabeth most certainly did not miss the exchange of glances and slight smiles between Maria and Georg. Her heart began to pound. Was it fear?

But she also felt excitement. It was almost like waiting for Tata to come home yesterday.

"We didn't see you this morning to hear the week's news," Georg said. "How are things with Lukas-Bátschi now home?"

What could Elisabeth say without speaking poorly about her father after only one day of having seen him again? But these were all close friends. She could probably find something to say that was honest but discreet.

"He told us last night about America, and how he believes what's happening there will affect us here." That should do it.

Stefan tilted his head to the side and crossed his arms. "I would love to hear more if you have time."

"Lissika has at least a few minutes," Maria answered for her. Elisabeth did not miss the hint of mischief in her friend's tone.

Of course Stefan would want to learn more. Wasn't that the type of man Elisabeth wanted to marry? But Tata's comments had also—at the dinner table, at least—involved Stefan, even if Tata hadn't known it.

Tata hadn't said anything specific about Stefan, so Elisabeth didn't have to say anything about that. "He saw a lot of factories."

Stefan nodded. "He worked in a cigar factory, didn't he?"

"Yes. But he saw lots of other factories. Shoe factories, for example."

Georg spoke. "A shoe factory or two in Romania would eventually put your father—and therefore Luki—out of business."

Elisabeth's tone saddened. "Tata actually thought factories might put blacksmiths out of business, too."

Georg didn't seem upset by this statement. "I agree with

him. Factories can make many tools and other metalworks much faster and easier than one or two men can."

Maria asked, "What about flour millers?"

"Tata believes they'll still be working for a while. A flour mill is not a factory, but it is like a machine. We don't grind flour by hand anymore, and my sisters and I don't know how to make thread from flax. We make our own wool, but we buy fabric for clothing and cotton thread for summer socks. So, some changes are maybe good. But how can a factory make shoes that fit really well?"

"It can't," Georg answered. "People will need to buy what fits them best. No different than the boots we had to wear during the war."

Elisabeth relaxed. Now the air between her and Stefan had calmed. Now, they all spoke as friends.

"Machines that will replace everything..." Stefan said. "That means men need to be able to work with them. Especially in factories, where quick work is needed." He glanced briefly at his empty sleeve and then at Elisabeth. In that moment, she knew what he was thinking: that no one would hire a man with only one arm, which meant he wouldn't be able to support a wife and family.

"I don't know if these changes will happen quickly," she added, hoping to say something comforting. "And Tata did say that farmers will always be needed."

Could Elisabeth somehow earn money? Day labourers earned a little money but were also paid through food, like bacon, flour, butter, and such. Elisabeth didn't have Mammi's skills at sewing. But she could draw...

She shook her head. No one would hire her to do something so frivolous.

"I have a feeling you're having a conversation with yourself," Stefan said. "I'd love to hear it."

Elisabeth let out a nervous giggle and then stopped herself. If she didn't act like a woman—composed and always mindful of her surroundings—Stefan would definitely not want to marry her. "I'm just wondering if I could somehow earn money. Like Mammi did."

"Did?" Georg asked. "She no longer embroiders shoes?"

"Tata won't let her. He said that it would look bad on him if his wife had to work to support the family. She's allowed to finish her current requests, but then she has to stop."

Stefan raised his eyebrows in surprise. "It says nothing of the sort. If anything, your mother's work shows how talented she is."

Elisabeth's heart skipped a beat.

"And how strong," Georg added. "Many people don't accept work from women unless it's to repair clothing."

Repair clothing. Elisabeth could do that. It wouldn't be enough income, she knew that much. But it would be a start. She was, after all, only fifteen. She might—if God allowed it—live another forty years, which was a long time to find ways to earn money.

"I don't know," Maria said. "I wouldn't want to work to earn money. Looking after the household and my children would make me happy."

"But what if your husband died?" Elisabeth asked. "You would need to be prepared to make money."

Maria shrugged. "I would just marry again."

Elisabeth didn't want to worry Maria with more questions, but they swam around in her mind: What if another war happened, and too many men died? What if she had to settle for a man who would pay more attention to his children from his first marriage than to her children? What if this new husband lived in another village? At least Hagel Konrad lived in Semlak.

"It sounds like you have everything planned," Elisabeth said, putting on a smile.

"I have to admit," Stefan said, "I would find comfort in knowing that my wife could get through life without me... should something really sad happen." He sighed. "But after fighting in the war and spending two years in a Siberian prisoner-of-war camp, I hope God will spare me any more pain."

Georg patted Stefan on the back to comfort his friend, something Elisabeth had never seen before. Georg was changing, and maybe his new role as a father was part of that.

"I hope God will spare you pain, too," Elisabeth replied.

She lifted the bag of sugar. "I had better return home before Mammi gets angry."

Stefan doffed his cap again, Georg nodded, and everyone said their goodbyes.

Stefan, though, held her gaze for longer than usual. Elisabeth was certain this time.

Once the men were out of earshot, Maria giggled. "He definitely wants to marry you!"

That uncomfortable sensation of fear and excitement returned. "Do you think so?"

"Lissika Schuhmacher, it's clear as day. The look in his eyes and the way he smiles at you..."

Part of Elisabeth wanted Maria to be right because that meant Elisabeth's feelings were right. But part of her wanted her best friend to be wrong: Elisabeth hadn't spoken to Tata yet, and Tata had clearly stated at the table yesterday that Elisabeth was to marry someone who could work with machines or something like that. Tata would probably refuse Stefan's request, even though he had helped the Schuhmachers so often.

They reached the road that led to Maria's property. She lived on more land in the village because of her father's mill. Although milling was a profession Tata would accept, Maria's brother was too young for Elisabeth.

After the girls made arrangements to bake the next day, they parted ways, and Elisabeth returned home. She placed the sugar on a shelf in the kitchen and switched out her clean apron for an older one suitable for housework.

As she grabbed a bowl to head out to the garden to harvest tomatoes for a salad for supper, Tata walked out of the front room, rubbing his eyes.

"Did you have another sleep?" Elisabeth asked.

"Your mother will think I'm useless if I keep resting this much."

"You just arrived yesterday. The journey must have been so hard." Elisabeth had no idea what it would be like to ride on a boat, but given how long her father's journey had been—she had traced his path in the encyclopedia when he'd left—it would not have been easy. A train to Temeswar would interest her. But a trip halfway around the world? She couldn't imagine.

Tata nodded. "I don't want to ride on a ship ever again. The little boat that helps us cross the Marosch River in the warmer months is fine. But a ship that takes me so far from land that I can't see any for days? I will never do that again."

"I looked up where you were going in the encyclopedia. It seemed scary to me, but also exciting."

Tata shook his head. "The more you know about the world, Lissika, the harder it is to live in it."

Elisabeth poured her father a glass of water from the pitcher. "That's not what I think. The more I learned, the more I could help others. Like Mammi." She handed him the glass.

Tata took a long drink and then wiped his other hand over his face. Elisabeth couldn't tell if he was feeling regret or frustration; his expression seemed to show both. "If I had been here, you wouldn't have needed to know that."

"But I'm glad I did—"

"How can learning about...something like that be good for you? I didn't think the encyclopedia would have something about *that* inside. How do they know who'll read it?" He glanced toward the front room, where the encyclopedia was kept. "Maybe I should get rid of it."

"No!" Elisabeth's hand flew to her mouth before she could say any more. She had not intended to react that strongly toward her father, but the fear of losing her only source of world knowledge terrified her. Since her father's departure, when she couldn't sleep at night, Elisabeth had read about other places in the world—like a country called China, for example, that you could reach if you travelled east for a very long time, past where Jesus had lived. She also learned more about Germany, where her ancestors came from.

Tata eyed her suspiciously. "What else have you been reading about?"

Elisabeth calmed herself before answering—it was probably best to list the topics he would approve of. "How blacksmithing works, how you travelled across the ocean. I read a little about the empire we used to belong to. I also tried to find out where Jesus lived."

At that last sentence, Tata smiled. "Maybe you have put your reading to good use." Tata headed toward the door. "I should go take over for your mother in the workshop."

"Eat first, Tata. Let me make you a snack."

He sat down at the kitchen table without objecting, and Elisabeth prepared smoked salami on bread with butter, served it to him, refilled his glass with water, asked if he needed anything else, and then headed outside herself to harvest tomatoes.

She had convinced Tata that her reading had been useful. Would she be able to do the same about Stefan?

Stefan would not object to Elisabeth reading about topics for women. Although Elisabeth was certain he wouldn't want to discuss *those* kinds of topics, she wouldn't want to discuss topics about a man's body with him or anyone else either. But if she wanted to read about China, or hear about what was happening in the world, Stefan would never tell her no, and in fact, he would ask for her opinion.

He was exactly the type of man she wanted.

CHAPTER NINE

The basement had become oddly crowded: Aunt Anne and Uncle Peter had to move around one another as they searched through Opa's room like sleuths. It left Juliana wondering if they'd done this kind of thing before. They carefully lifted items out of the way to search, then made sure everything was put back exactly as it had been. Juliana, Rachel, and Sophie stayed outside the bedroom, each trying to watch over the other's shoulder.

"Oh my god, what's this?" Uncle Peter held up a woman's braid.

Aunt Anne laughed. "That's Modr's hair."

Uncle Peter yelped as he let it drop.

Aunt Anne picked it up as though it were a treasure. "Peter! A lot of women save their braids if they cut off all their hair. I'd forgotten Tata had this." She paused and stared at the long brown braid. "She had cut it off by the time you were little—she'd noticed that a lot of women cut their hair when they got older, so she followed suit."

"Older? She was only thirty-six when I was born."

Aunt Anne set the braid back in the drawer. "Back then, they would say someone that age was moving into the second half of her life." She laughed. "Or maybe you were such a handful that she cut off her hair because you kept pulling it."

Uncle Peter crossed his arms. "Or I was so charming that she saw the silver lining that came with me: I'd keep her young."

Aunt Anne snorted. "I've never heard anyone refer to a baby who spits up everywhere as charming."

Then Aunt Anne sighed as she closed the drawer. "Nothing," she said. "I think we're out of options."

"Wait a minute," Juliana said. "Opa's drawers have liners at the bottom. Did you look under those? If he's hiding something but can't find it, underneath those liners would fit the bill."

No sooner did Aunt Anne open a drawer and lift the liner than she exclaimed, "I think we found them!"

Juliana jumped up and down, Sophie clapped her hands, and Rachel hugged them both.

"But wait," Sophie asked. "'Them'?"

Within a few minutes, Aunt Anne and Uncle Peter had

retrieved a small stack of photos from each drawer in the dresser and held them out to the girls.

"He's got at least twelve or thirteen here," Uncle Peter said.

There she was: the same woman—her clothes changing, her face aging—in each photo. The last few, in which she looked maybe just a little younger than Opa was now, were in colour.

Juliana's breath caught. Elisabeth had hazel eyes, high cheekbones, and what Juliana could best describe as a sturdy build. But looking at her great-grandmother beside some of the men... Either the men were really tall, or Elisabeth was short. In some of the photos, she smiled kindly. In others, her expression was more serious.

So, this is my friend, Juliana thought.

Aunt Anne and Uncle Peter quickly reset Opa's room while the girls stared at each photo in turn, and then everyone headed upstairs and pulled out a chair around the kitchen table.

Juliana retrieved the book of drawings from her backpack, which she'd thrown into the kitchen when they'd arrived. Everyone pored over the drawings and the photos.

Juliana stared at a photo of Elisabeth and a man who looked a little older than her. His arm was missing. "This is her wedding photo."

Uncle Peter turned it around. "Oh my god, Annie, look. Something's written on the back."

They turned all the photos around, and each one had the same handwriting.

"That's not Tata's writing," Aunt Anne said.

Juliana couldn't read the words, but the writing looked beautiful and graceful. "...Like an artist's handwriting," Juliana said, finishing her thought out loud. "What if this is Elisabeth's handwriting?"

Uncle Peter read slowly. "This looks like German, but it also doesn't. Give me a couple of minutes." After what seemed like eternity to Juliana as she waited, Uncle Peter let out a nervous laugh. "You're all staring at me."

"We want answers!" Juliana said, her voice filled with excitement.

Then she heard the sound of the side door being unlocked. Juliana held her breath as Mom came in with Opa.

How would he react? Should Juliana pull out the ingredients for a sandwich for him to try to keep him calm?

Rachel touched her wrist and whispered, "One step at a time. Just like how we learn our routines in dance class."

The advice immediately calmed Juliana.

At first, Opa was surprised. "All my children are here! I love to see you all like this." Then he noticed the girls. "Sophie! And Rachel—so nice that you visit us."

"Thank you for letting me stay, Mr. Schuhmacher."

Opa waved away the compliment. "Yulika's friends are always welcome in my house."

Mom helped Opa slip out of his shoes, and he joined them at the table. His eyes opened wide again. "You found it?"

Now Juliana was confused.

But Opa reached for one particular photo, turned it around, read the back, and nodded. "This is my father. I don't remember him. But Modr insisted on one photo of the three of us before she and I left for Semlak. He had a job in a factory in Temeswar and didn't want to leave." He took a deep breath and let it out. "She told me when I was older that he died shortly after we left. From an accident in the factory."

The black-and-white photo had ornate buildings in the background. In the foreground stood a young man—with two arms—a woman about the same age, and a little boy, maybe three years old.

Opa pointed to the boy and laughed. "That's me. Can you recognize me?"

Rachel cooed. "You look so cute, Mr. Schuhmacher."

Opa ran his hand over his mostly bald head. "I had more hair."

The atmosphere in the kitchen relaxed.

"But why this photo, Tata?" Mom asked. "And why keep all these separate from your other ones?"

Opa took a while to study each photo and read the back. "After Modr died, we cleaned up her things. Tante Anna and I found these. We knew Modr was trying to pass on knowledge of her family to me." He sighed heavily. "When I knew you and your family were moving in with me, I put them somewhere safe." He raised a finger. "I trust all of you! But when many people live in a small house, accidents can happen."

That made sense to Juliana. These were his treasures. It was too bad, though, that he'd forgotten where he'd put them. Juliana had longed all these months to see what her great-grandmother had looked like.

"Can you read the back of each one?" Uncle Peter asked. "I'm trying to, but I can't make out all the words, even though the handwriting is so neat."

Opa nodded. "Modr learned Romanian and some German in school, but spelling was always hard for her. I remember she spoke out loud when she wrote. I think she wanted to hear the word and then spell it. Some of her writing uses words from German, and some from Romanian, and some words use both languages."

"A learning disability?" Aunt Anne asked.

Opa shrugged. "I don't know about such things. Modr read lots of books. I know that."

"But she couldn't spell," Mom said. She looked at the backs of some of the photos. "I guess we'll never know for sure."

"What do they say?" Uncle Peter asked.

Opa read each one out loud to his family. Juliana learned that her great-grandmother had three siblings—

and one photo Opa said was from the 1930s had four adults in it: Elisabeth, two sisters, and one brother. Opa pointed to the one: "She was smart. A good head on her shoulders. That's why we named you after her, Annie," he said to his oldest daughter.

"But one thing you've never told us, Tata," Mom said, "was why you carry your mother's last name."

Opa folded his hands and closed his eyes.

Mom rubbed his back. "I didn't mean to upset you. We don't have to talk about it."

"I don't remember everything Tante Anna told me about the pictures. I don't want to die and know my family doesn't know everything about their ancestors." He paused to collect his thoughts. "Mammi didn't want to marry a second time. She said my father was a nice man, but he wouldn't move to a village like Semlak. He was happy with his job in a factory in Temeswar." He paused. "She never talked about her first husband other than to say he was very, very kind and that he stood up for what was right. But any time she talked about him when I was young, she began to cry, so I stopped asking. All I know is that he died trying to protect some people from...I guess you say 'bullies' today. It was the 1930s." He picked up the wedding photo, read the back, and nodded. "They were married for seventeen years. They had children, but I never knew them. I think they passed away. Mammi always said I was her only child." He shook his head. "Life was so hard for her."

Only now did he look up, his eyes red. "Because my life has been so wonderful, and Mammi's so hard, I carried a photo of her in my pocket to remind me that I can get through this." He pointed to his head.

Juliana heard some sniffling, and both Rachel and Sophie were crying. That broke Juliana's dam, and she passed them both the tissue box first before pulling a few out for herself.

He held up the photo of his parents. "*Danke. Danke, danke, danke,*" he said, looking around the circle at the table.

"Thank Juliana," Aunt Anne said. "She knew where to look. I hope you don't mind that Peter and I went through your things." She explained where she'd found the photos, and Opa's eyes widened.

"That's where I put them!" He pointed to his head. "Stupid roof damage. I wanted to make sure I didn't lose them."

Opa stood up and gave Juliana the tightest hug she'd ever felt from him. "*Danke* so much." He proceeded to slide the photo into his pants pocket.

"Wait, Opa!"

Her exuberance startled her grandfather. "What is it?"

"Why don't we put it in a frame for you? That way, it can stay on your dresser in your bedroom and not get lost in the wash."

Opa thought about Juliana's idea for a moment, but he

shook his head. His voice became quiet as he answered. "I need this photo with me."

Juliana had another idea. "Opa, did you know that you can make copies of a photo really fast today?"

"What do you mean?"

She struggled to find the words—how could she explain to her grandfather what scanning and printing on photo paper meant?

"Like a photocopier," Mom interjected. "Do you remember—sometimes Peter, Annie, and I had to make copies of projects for school? We'd go to the library and use a special machine?"

Opa's eyes brightened. "Yes! Yes, I do! You can do that with pictures?"

Aunt Anne nodded. "I can do it tomorrow for you, Tata. We have a machine like that in our house. I can make a few copies, and we'll put the original in a frame, like Juliana said."

Opa happily handed the photo to his daughter, tears forming in his eyes. "Thank you," he said. "Be careful with it."

"I can get frames on my way home from work tomorrow," Mom offered.

Once plans were finalized, Opa thanked everyone again. Then he walked over to the drawer in the small counter beside the fridge, pulled out his wallet, and gave Juliana forty dollars.

"You and Sophie and Rachel go have something nice to eat," he said.

Uncle Peter huffed his indignation and playfully complained, "What about your children?"

Opa laughed. "You all have jobs."

Suddenly Juliana exclaimed, "My report!" She had told herself she'd spend two hours searching before starting her project, but looking at the clock, it had been closer to four.

"You haven't started yet?" Mom asked.

Even Opa had something to say about the matter. "Yulika, thank you very much for the pictures. But your school comes first."

Rachel leaned across Juliana to Sophie. "I guess we're checking out the tea shop?"

Sophie and Rachel high-fived in front of Juliana. Each grabbed one of her hands and yanked her onto her feet.

"Get your notebook!" Rachel said.

Juliana was not amused when everyone laughed.

CHAPTER TEN

The organ played and everyone rose as the pastor, dressed in his black cassock and white surplice, entered from the side door of the church to begin the service.

Elisabeth's family sat in their customary positions: Tata with the men, Mammi with the women, and her siblings in the balcony. Omama sat in the front row with the older women.

Elisabeth, now confirmed but not married, sat in a special place to the right of the altar, in the small collection of pews, where everyone could see which young people were still not married. Before her confirmation, Elisabeth had been excited for the moment when she could sit up there until marriage. Afterwards, though, she realized how uncomfortable this could make someone feel.

The older you get, the farther up you sit in the congregation, she thought. *Except when you're waiting for a husband or wife. Then you're beside the pastor.*

A few of the young men and women with her were now eighteen or nineteen years old. Elisabeth knew better than to ask how they felt, but she could well imagine that they would prefer to be sitting with the married couples in the nave.

She continued to sing with the congregation, enjoying this peaceful time when everyone got along with each other as they rejoiced in God. Jesus did teach that God accepted everyone who followed the Ten Commandments, did He not?

Eva, her new baby in her arms, sat beside Margarethe-Néni, who frequently glanced toward the men. Was she looking at Georg? Stefan? Or where Konrad-Bátschi used to sit? Elisabeth didn't want to stare to find out. Someone would say something about that later.

After the pastor gave his customary greetings, everyone sat and the service began.

The sea of black-and-white linen spread itself out before Elisabeth. *Everyone is dressed almost the same,* she thought. She had always known that—even dreamed of the day she would receive her black clothing, which was only for married women. But only now did she realize that many in the congregation also thought the same way as one another. They all ridiculed Georg—sitting at the end of a pew, his back against the wall—gossiped about the young men and women sitting around Elisabeth, said rude things to Mammi—as Elisabeth knew because Mammi told her—about Elisabeth cutting her bangs like Maria, and more. Yes, they had different opinions of what made a good gulasch or torte, or how someone should embroider butterflies on a handkerchief, but for all the important matters in life—birth, confirmation, marriage, even death—they all thought the same.

The only exceptions in clothing were the children in the balcony and those sitting with Elisabeth. Their Sunday best was a little different, especially for the young, confirmed women who now could wear colourful skirts and beautifully embroidered tops to further announce that they hadn't yet married. Even though young wives still dressed in colourful clothing for dances and other formal events, they wore their black *tschirak* and skirt, with a black kerchief, to church.

Maria leaned over and whispered, "Stefan's been watching you."

Elisabeth turned her head in time to see Stefan look back at the pastor. Her cheeks heated up. When she returned her attention to Pastor Fröhlich, she caught Maria's knowing smile out of the corner of her eye.

Elisabeth's insides churned like cream being made into

butter. Today, she would formally introduce Tata and Stefan after the service.

The next time the congregation stood, Elisabeth looked in Stefan's direction again, and he caught her eye. He smiled, held her gaze, gave her an almost invisible nod, and then looked ahead to the pastor and the altar.

Elisabeth's body heated up. One glance at Tata, though, cooled her right down: he must have caught the exchange between her and Stefan, and he did not look pleased.

Elisabeth bowed her head, pretending to recite the prayer everyone else was saying, but instead whispered her own, "Please, Jesus, give me the strength to convince my father to let me marry Stefan. He's kind, gentle, will allow me to keep reading and learning about the world, and he helps wherever he can. He is the man I want for a husband."

As everyone filed out at the end of the service, Maria squeezed her hand. "Are you ready?"

"I don't know." Elisabeth kept her voice as low as possible, knowing full well that others would try to listen in on her conversation. "Tata wants me to marry someone who can work with machines and do jobs like the ones he saw in America."

"But surely Americans have farms?" They followed the rest of the congregation. "How else can you make food?"

"But he has no land, just his parents' house in the village. His parents are day labourers, and his sister is not well. Stefan lost his brother in the war, so we would have to look after Magdalena, too. Then there's the matter with… his arm. You've said so yourself."

They stepped into the bright Sunday sunlight. Stefan and his parents were discussing something while his sister —who rarely stayed after church service—stood in silence, staring at the ground.

"But you convinced me otherwise," Maria said.

"You're not a father looking to marry off his first daughter."

"No, but I was trying to look out for you. When you helped me see how he will look after you, I changed my mind. Your father also wants to make sure you'll be cared for. So, Lissika, convince him of that."

Elisabeth caught Stefan's eye, and he left his family to come to her side.

Only now did Elisabeth see just how polished he looked, from his tall, shiny, black boots, to his ironed pants and shirt, lint-free black vest, and cleanly cut hair.

Should she compliment him on his appearance? How did one act with a man one wanted to marry? Before she could even answer her own question, Maria elbowed her in the back.

Elisabeth stammered. "You, you look very nice today."

Stefan's smile reached from ear to ear. "And you look lovely."

The only reaction Elisabeth could muster was a giggle.

"Good morning, Stefan," Maria said. "It's a beautiful day, isn't it?"

"It is. Will you be at the Schuhmachers this afternoon?"

Maria nodded. "I helped bake." She patted Elisabeth on the shoulder. "Lissika is helping me become a better house-wife for Konrad. She's very good at it."

Elisabeth wanted to swat Maria. How rude was it to boast, even if you were not the one boasting?

"I do like your baking," he said to Elisabeth.

All right. Your only choices are to continue feeling as hot as the sun while your best friend tries to embarrass you, Elisabeth thought, *or you can introduce the man you like to your father.*

"Let's go," she said.

Maria laughed. "In a hurry?"

When would Elisabeth stop acting so strangely around Stefan?

"We'll see you this afternoon, then," Stefan said to Maria.

We? Who was "we"?

Elisabeth and Stefan crossed the church yard to where her father was talking with a few other men in the commu-nity, including Meier Josef.

What new rumours was Meier Josef spreading today?

"Tata?" Elisabeth's voice squeaked. This was not a good start. If she was going to convince her father that Stefan was her choice, she needed to show more confidence.

But before she could make another attempt, her father turned and smiled at her. "I can see that you know your prayers. You studied hard for your confirmation."

Elisabeth nodded and thanked him for his compliment. "Tata...this is...this is..."

Stefan held out his left hand. "Schäfer Stefan," he said with the confidence Elisabeth was missing.

Tata first held out his right hand and then corrected himself. His expression of disapproval was brief but clear to Elisabeth. Tata remained civil, but he was not personable as he had just been with the other men.

That was neither polite nor fair.

"Tata, Stefan has helped out a lot at the *salasch* and at home. He also built the small stove in the workshop."

Tata nodded, acknowledging what she'd said. "Lissika wrote to me about that. Thank you very much for your help with my family while I was away."

"It was no problem at all."

Tata indicated to Stefan's missing arm. "War?"

Stefan nodded. "A bomb went off beside me when we stormed the enemy line. Then I was captured and sent to a camp."

Tata pressed his lips together, his eyes sad. "The war was hard on all of us," he said.

"I understand you made boots for us soldiers. That might explain why they were so comfortable."

Tata smiled a little. "At least in the beginning." He looked at Elisabeth and paused. "The war is over. Let it die with those of us who fought so that the rest of you can live with happy memories."

Elisabeth, her hand pressed into her full skirt, formed a fist. Georg and Stefan had already shared with her stories about what they had seen; why Georg had his nightmares; how the soldiers had less and less food as the war raged on. She'd also already known how Stefan had lost his arm. To Elisabeth, this war was harder on the soldiers than Jesus's crucifixion must have been on Him. *Please forgive me if I'm wrong*, she thought. But these men spent sometimes several years huddled in huts while snow fell without mercy and ice formed on their hair and moustaches. Men tried to pull back dead bodies from the place of battle so they could be buried properly, endangering themselves while they did so. Or they could develop a sickness and die, sometimes slowly and painfully because they didn't always have doctors or the right medicines.

It was hell on Earth. And Tata wanted to keep the truth from her.

"Those were difficult times." Stefan nodded to Tata. How he said so politely what he had gone through filled Elisabeth with wonder. "It was nice to meet you, Herr Schuhmacher. I look forward to this afternoon. I understand Lissika has done some wonderful baking."

Tata smiled and nodded back. "She has learned a lot

since I left." But Elisabeth picked up a tone in his voice that said he disapproved of some of her learning. Her stomach tightened. What had happened to the father who'd supported her efforts to learn more than what school had taught her? The one who'd encouraged her to read the encyclopedia so she could better understand this big world they lived in?

The one who'd wanted her to keep a journal of drawings so he could see all the important events that had happened in his absence? He hadn't even asked to see it yet, and it had already been four days since his arrival. Even showing him a few drawings once after supper would have made her happy. But instead, Tata had taken Luki under his wing.

Stefan doffed his cap to her and returned to his family. As Elisabeth watched him cross the lawn, she noticed many people staring back at her. Was she now the subject of village gossip because everyone knew Tata would not approve of a man with such an injury? She hated to think what everyone was saying about her behind her back. What business was it of theirs? Should she ask Pastor Fröhlich to talk about the evils of gossip next week? People listened to what he said.

Tata had returned to talking with his friends.

Why had he refused to continue talking about the boots? Elisabeth had to find out, or she wouldn't be able to focus on her tasks this afternoon.

She sought out Georg's company, since that would hopefully raise fewer eyebrows, and asked him.

"When resources began to run out," he said, "soldiers had to use boots from their fellow fallen soldiers."

Elisabeth's stomach rose to her throat. Wear a dead man's boots? Tata had never spoken about that.

Some of what Elisabeth had learned this past year had weighed heavily on her—like this great war—or had embarrassed her—like learning about what was happening to a woman who had a baby inside her. But all of it had helped Elisabeth become a more loving, compassionate person.

Was that not what a Christian should try to become? she asked herself.

Tata had spoken about the pains of the war, but he didn't seem to understand the pain in Elisabeth's heart because of how he was treating Stefan.

Maybe Stefan also reminds Tata about the war, and that's why he doesn't want me to marry him, she thought. She'd learned this year that Mammi sometimes acted angrily when she was sad, like when she'd lost the baby. Georg had even warned Elisabeth about that.

Was Tata doing something like that?

Maria was right. Elisabeth had to convince her father that Stefan was the man she should be allowed to marry. Not only had he helped her become the woman she now was, but he would continue to make her a better person because he would allow her to keep learning. All this time, Elisabeth had believed that Tata had moved on from the war. Instead, she now saw that he still relived it in his own way. Maybe not with nightmares like Georg, or an injury to his body like Stefan, but he still felt it deeply inside his heart.

CHAPTER ELEVEN

The three girls stood across the street from Claire's Tea Shop, waiting for the crosswalk to activate. Modern signs and storefronts covered most of the original red-brick building. From where she stood, Juliana couldn't see any customers at the tables. Hopefully, they would be alone with Pauline: Juliana didn't want to hear anyone ask her about such an embarrassing career.

She glanced at her notebook, thankful that Rachel and Sophie had let her take twenty minutes to watch a few quick videos about Pauline's career and write down some questions. She read one to the girls as they waited. "How dumb is this: 'Why did you become a mascot actor?' Clearly, the answer has to be for money. Who would take on such embarrassing work?"

"How do you know what she'll answer?" Sophie shook

her head. "For someone who loves learning, it's weird you're not looking forward to talking to this woman. She's done some amazing things!"

Juliana couldn't argue there: Pauline, in those big costumes, would jump off a trampoline and do a slam dunk into a basketball net. Or she'd play a hockey game with other mascot actors, and they actually sometimes scored or kept the puck out of the net. The newspaper article they'd found about her said she was the only woman working as a mascot actor in the professional men's hockey league at that time. That did sound kind of cool, too. But that still wasn't enough to change Juliana's mind.

"I find mascots kind of freaky. You have no idea who's staring back at you, and they don't talk."

The light changed, and they crossed. Juliana took a deep breath and opened the door. She relaxed when she saw a young man wiping down equipment behind the counter and not Pauline. Maybe she could push this off another few days.

Then the young man turned around. Wait a minute... Austin Tschirhart?

Before her brain could shut off the flow of words, Juliana blurted out, "Oh my god—you're the reason I came to Kitchener Dance Academy!"

Austin had just graduated from both Eby Heights and Kitchener Dance Academy. Rumour had it he would soon be joining an apprenticeship program with a professional ballet company in British Columbia. Juliana had started following him on social media as soon as she discovered he danced there.

Austin's cheeks immediately turned the colour of cherries, and he ran a hand through his brown hair. "I don't know what to say. Thank you. That's a first for me, Juliana."

Juliana's jaw dropped. "You know my name?" *Probably because I keep messing up.*

"You were a new face in the middle of the year, and Jasmine told me you've been practising a lot. I could see it during our year-end recital."

Now Juliana's cheeks heated up. Austin used dance to make the world a better place: he spoke out against bullying, used his platform to create awareness for epilepsy, a condition he lived with, and to encourage anyone anywhere to dance. He had around seventy-five thousand followers.

Juliana had maybe two hundred. Total.

A woman came out from the back room and smiled at the girls. She was older—well, about the same age as Mom and Aunt Anne. Her sleeveless blouse showed very muscular arms. Her short, brown hair had grey streaks in it. Juliana recognized her face from the online footage and article they had looked at.

"Another fan, Austin?"

Could this get worse? The last impression Juliana

wanted to leave Pauline with was that she was fangirling over Austin.

"This is Pauline," Austin said. "The owner."

"Perfect!" Rachel said. Juliana jumped at her sudden reaction.

Pauline smiled. "I'm guessing I'm wanted? Is it a good thing or a bad thing?"

Rachel pushed Juliana ahead of her. "It's your project."

Introductions were always a good way to start, right? "I'm, well, doing a school project. I'm Juliana. I dance. At Kitchener Dance Academy and go to Eby Heights. And this is Sophie, my cousin, and Rachel, my best friend from back home."

"Calgary," Rachel added.

How could I forget that important detail? Juliana asked herself. She broke into a sweat. Besides feeling stupid talking to a mascot actor, she found Pauline's stature slightly intimidating. But now that she had taken the first step for this project, she had to follow through.

"I'm...I'm doing a school project. About jobs. Careers. And...Mr. Casimiro said yours was...is...was really interesting." *Great. Now she'll think I'm unprepared*, she thought.

"The grade ten careers course?" Austin asked.

Juliana nodded, her voice having flown out the front door. How could she ask anything intelligent if she was this nervous?

Pauline gestured to a table. "Happy to help if I can. Please have a seat. Anything we can get you to eat? Drink?"

"We have *the best* chocolate brownies," Austin said. "They're from my mom and Ben's store, the chocolate shop?"

All three girls' jaws dropped, but Rachel found her voice first. "A chocolate shop?! Why haven't we gone there?"

Juliana sheepishly shrugged. "Casimiro's became mine and Sophie's regular place, and you only got here Saturday..."

Everyone laughed and Austin fulfilled their orders: iced rooibos lemon tea because it sounded interesting, and three chocolate brownies.

Pauline invited them to sit down with her and opened the conversation by asking them more about themselves. Juliana's nerves began to settle. There was something inviting about this woman's presence.

Austin walked over with everyone's orders, including a steaming tea for Pauline that smelled like cranberries, if Juliana had to name the scent.

"So?" Pauline asked. "What did you want to know?"

Juliana froze again. "Um..." She opened her notebook and stared at the basic questions.

Rachel jumped in. "We saw some of the cool stuff you did online. How did you learn all that?"

Juliana silently thanked her best friend and prepared to take notes.

They learned that Pauline had studied gymnastics until she was maybe fourteen, and that those skills helped her entertain kids when she babysat. Her degree in psychology helped her better understand people. She acted first for party companies and later for a huge amusement park in Florida. "I actually once wore one of those pink gorilla suits for a video store in the summer and held a sign that pointed people to the store." She laughed. "Worst job ever, let me tell you. But I almost always found work for sports teams—sometimes volunteer, often paid. That was the best: getting fans riled up so they could cheer the team and boost team morale, that was an incredible feeling."

So this had been a true career for her. Juliana still couldn't imagine why, or how she could include this information in her report without her teacher laughing at her. She was certain her teacher would prefer she write about becoming a doctor or an accountant or something like that.

But Juliana was here now. She might as well find out whatever she could. "Do you mind my asking...why you enjoyed it?" Would Pauline be insulted by the question?

Instead of looking angry or put out, Pauline's face lit up in a knowing smile. "You're definitely not the first person to ask me that. Those costumes are super hot. A couple of years ago, I had to do the Peregrines' victory parade in the heat of July while basically wearing a full-body parka. I wore a cooling vest, and I held the straw of my hydration pack in my mouth for two hours, but I was still boiling.

And I loved it. When I wore a costume, I became more comfortable with myself and much more outgoing."

That last answer Juliana hadn't expected. In her mind, wearing one of those costumes would make her shyer*f*.

"I kind of feel like that when I wear a dance costume and put on stage makeup," Rachel said. "It's not the same kind of costume, but putting on something sparkly, something special so you can impress judges, the audience, whoever's watching—it feels really good."

Austin joined in the conversation from behind the counter. "I feel the same way. Nothing beats putting on sparkling clean white tights, a beautifully made—sometimes hand-embroidered—top, and trying to give audiences the performance they've been expecting."

Juliana had to admit that all made sense. But dance costumes were usually designed to allow the dancer to move easily and show off their abilities. A big, fluffy costume seemed somewhat restricting, not to mention making it impossible to see or hear very well.

"Can you...do you mind telling more about that? How did being..." *Dressed up* sounded rude, as though Pauline was talking about Halloween fun. "How did being in such a big costume make you more confident and outgoing?"

Pauline took a sip of her tea before answering. "I had tons of energy in my youth. My sister even wore headphones to try to drown me out when I used our house as a parkour course." Everyone laughed. "But by the time I was in high school, I'd already hit six feet. So, where some girls were, you know, growing out, I had grown up. I was skinny as a rail, and boys ignored me completely. At about the same time, my gymnastics coach told me I'd grown too tall to compete."

Sophie sat up straight. "You weren't allowed to compete because you didn't have the right kind of body?"

Pauline nodded as she took another sip of her tea. "My self-esteem plummeted. I understand things now—the benefits of age. Just look at Simone Biles. She's four-foot-eight. I wouldn't be able to come even near to what she can do." Pauline had a point. "So, I turned to lifting weights. Seemed like something I could do with the body I had. Modelling certainly wasn't my thing. And feeling how I did about myself, team sports like volleyball and basketball intimidated me."

Juliana hadn't expected someone with Pauline's stature and demeanour to feel like that.

Pauline continued. "When the student who'd acted as our high school mascot quit, my best friend—Austin's mom —told me to try out." Pauline smiled the way Opa did when he got lost in a memory. "No one saw the tall, skinny-as-rail Pauline. They saw a character who excited them enough to cheer for their team. Sure, some made fun of me, but it didn't matter. I wasn't me: I was that character. But at the same time, I finally felt comfortable with myself again."

"I guess that's kind of like how I feel better when I've had time to dance," Juliana said.

"Austin's the same. Aren't you?"

"The worst time in my life was when I stopped dancing," he said from behind the counter. "I really locked myself away. It felt like I was standing on a dark stage, the curtains closed, lights down, and no one there except me."

"You were pretty angry," Pauline said.

"And lonely," he added. "You helped me find my way out."

"You did all the work."

"But someone had to open the door."

Knowing what Juliana did about Austin, it had never occurred to her just how powerful the arts could be—in any form. He had shared a video online from a couple of years ago where he'd danced a duet at Eby Heights with the Toronto Peregrines' mascot—back then, Pauline—and talked about how that performance had given him the strength to return to dance. Only this time, he'd speak out louder for people like him—people who lived with stigma.

Juliana now knew one person Pauline had helped. How many more were there? Probably thousands in some way, shape, or form. All through acting.

The bell over the door rang, a customer entered, and Austin turned to serve him.

Pauline continued. "If everyone had an outlet like dance or acting or music...anything—"

"Drawing," Juliana added, thinking of Elisabeth.

Pauline nodded in agreement. "Anything that gives your thoughts and feelings a way out. There'd be so much more empathy in the world because people would be more in tune with themselves. They'd understand what emotions do, how they make you feel and think and act. That's my opinion, anyway."

Juliana scribbled that down. She'd had no idea this conversation would go in this direction. Maybe sometimes flying by the seat of your pants actually worked.

As the conversation with Pauline continued, Juliana learned that professional mascot actors could find themselves in sad situations. For example, Pauline sometimes had to hold the hand of a terminally ill child.

"I don't know how you did that," Juliana said, full of awe. "When I performed at an old age home and saw so many people my grandfather's age and older..." She took in a deep breath as the memory returned to her. "I had a panic attack. Mom thought something was wrong. So did I. I didn't realize that seeing so many people..." She fought for the right words, because she didn't want to come across as mean. "So many sick people like that would scare me."

Rachel said, "It took you a couple of weeks to tell me that, didn't it?"

Sophie added, "And me."

As the full memory of that time in the winter returned, Juliana remembered why. "I felt like I'd seen how Opa's life was going to end. This sounds stupid now, but I thought if I didn't say anything, the rest of his life would be happy."

Pauline leaned forward, her expression earnest. "Not stupid at all, Juliana. Everyone needs time to think things through before talking about really difficult topics. If you can find a way to combine those difficult experiences with your love for dance, and in a way that's safe for you, I think you'd find a powerful and fulfilling career for yourself."

Juliana was almost ready to hug Pauline, even without the costume. She had no idea such compassionate people could be underneath all that fleece.

"I guess that's like how Opa didn't tell any of us about his photo," Sophie said. She quickly explained the situation to Pauline, and Juliana watched a range of emotions appear on the actor's face.

"People share their emotions in their own time," Pauline said. "I don't know how many told me they weren't ready to talk to a loved one yet about something, but they needed to tell someone. Since I was completely anonymous, they spoke to me."

Having finished with his customer, Austin rejoined them. "Juliana probably wants to know what kind of career planning you did. She'll needed it for her report."

So, my question wasn't stupid, she thought. *Note to self: just ask the question.*

"Careers can happen by happenstance," Pauline said.

"No amount of career planning in high school would've prepped me for this life."

Juliana scribbled that down and double-underlined it. "But if you enjoyed it so much, why do you run the tea shop now?"

Pauline explained the history of her career transition while Juliana wrote everything down as fast as she could. After another ten minutes of talking, Juliana profusely thanked Pauline for her time, and Sophie and Rachel echoed her sentiments.

On the way back home, Sophie asked what Juliana thought about it all.

"I'm actually..." She smiled. "I'm glad you two forced me to do this. It was fascinating." Sophie and Rachel high-fived each other. "I have a feeling my paper is going to go in a direction I didn't plan...and that's okay. I can't wait to write this."

CHAPTER TWELVE

osina fell to the ground, tears streaming down her cheeks as she wailed.

She had dropped three forks onto the kitchen floor.

"Rosina, please!" Elisabeth pleaded with her. "You'll get your dress all dirty!"

If she'd dropped the cutlery in the back room, she might have fallen onto the area rug that lay on the floor. But the dirt floors in the kitchen and front room were bare.

"Wash them quickly. No need to cry about this." Elisabeth happily supported her siblings where she could, but they had to learn to take responsibility for their mistakes, too.

"They have to be perfect for Tata!" Rosina rolled onto her side, tears now streaming sideways down her face and leaving wet drops on the floor.

Elisabeth sighed and prayed to Jesus for patience. Rosina went from being scared of her father to wanting to do everything and anything to impress him.

All within four days.

Anna brought over a stack of cups and saucers to Rosina. "Take these to the front room." She picked up the strewn cutlery.

Rosina sat up, wiped her eyes and nose with her hands, eyed the cups and saucers, and stood up. She reached out her hands, and Elisabeth raced to the other side of the kitchen to get a cloth and wipe them before she touched anything. Mammi always said not to touch clean dishes with dirty hands, that no one wanted dishes that looked like they'd been stored in the animal stalls.

"Be careful, Rosina!" Elisabeth called out to her sister. *I should check her underskirts to be sure*, she thought, but she knew people would be arriving shortly. Elisabeth didn't have time to help Rosina change.

"Thank you," she said to Anna.

"I noticed at school that when little kids get upset and someone asks them to do something else, they often stop crying right away."

How did Elisabeth not know that after raising her own siblings since Christmas? Now that she thought about it, she had used this trick on occasion, especially with Luki, but it had never occurred to her that it was a real way to handle younger children.

If her younger sister could figure something like this out, what did that mean for Elisabeth's desire to have her own family? Would she be a good mother?

A knock on the door signalled the first arrivals. Elisabeth couldn't have been happier to see Maria, her parents and brother carrying additional dishes.

And even a *hefezopf*.

"Oh my goodness! Thank you so much, Frau Haibach!" As Elisabeth took the braided sweet bread, she could immediately smell its poppy seed filling. She set it on the central table in the kitchen among the other desserts she had baked: cookies with white icing decorations, a strawberry torte, a coffee cake, and, of course, her rum roll. It had turned out beautifully.

Frau Haibach, always friendly, nodded. "Maria told me you'd forgotten to buy enough yeast. I hope your father likes this."

"Tata will love it. Even though he lived among other Semlakers in America, he said the baking never tasted quite the same."

Frau Haibach offered to help, but Elisabeth insisted she didn't have to. "Besides, I think Mammi would like some company. She's cleaning the outdoor kitchen." *But probably also enjoying a moment or two alone with Tata,* Elisabeth thought.

"Cleaning it so it's more than clean?" Frau Haibach asked.

Elisabeth nodded. "I would be grateful if you could distract her." She also pointed Herr Haibach and Maria's brother back outside to join Tata.

Maria took a deep breath. "Is that coffee I smell, Lissika?"

"Oh no!" If the coffee brewed too long, it would taste bitter. She didn't want to waste the coffee Tata had brought back from America, where it was much cheaper than here. She had been too focused on Rosina!

As she rushed to the stove, she let out a little yelp: one of the forks Rosina had dropped still lay on the ground and had pushed into the bottom of her house shoe.

She picked it up and moaned. "Look at that dent in the floor, Maria."

A voice coming from the door asked, "Is everything all right?"

Elisabeth whipped her head around to see Stefan peeking in. "Yes...yes, everything's fine... Hello."

He couldn't see her all disorderly like this. Could she hide the dent in the floor? Elisabeth and Anna had worked very hard yesterday to rub away all dents from the week, so that their loam-and-chaff floors looked immaculately smooth. Would Stefan think twice about marrying her if he believed Elisabeth had missed part of the floor?

But instead, he laughed when he entered and saw the floor. "Where do you keep your sand, cloths, and water?"

"Water?" Maria asked, seemingly as unsure of his request as Elisabeth was.

He nodded. "I'll rub that out for you."

Maria's jaw dropped so far that Elisabeth thought she might need to lift it up for her again. Except that she probably had the same expression on her own face.

Stefan laughed. "We did everything in the camp. I don't mind helping wherever I'm needed."

Still staring at him, Elisabeth pointed to the cupboard underneath the shelves, where she kept a bag of fine sand and thick cloths that wouldn't wear down fast from rubbing at the floor. Stefan helped himself and then indicated to a basin of water on the small table next to the shelving. "This water?"

Elisabeth nodded silently again.

"The coffee!" Maria shouted, startling Elisabeth.

When would she ever learn? She rushed to the stove—mindful to not trip over Stefan—and pulled the cooking pot off.

"That coffee smells wonderful," he said as he scrubbed.

"I don't know if it's been cooking too long," she said.

"Just add a little sugar, Lissika. No one will know." Stefan smiled at her and again held eye contact with her. When he turned back to face the floor, Maria silently squealed—if one could do that—and placed both hands over her heart.

Her cheeks as hot as the coffee in the pot, Elisabeth

took an old clean rag, stretched it over the coffee pot she had carefully washed the day before for the first time in three or four years, and tipped the cooking pot over the cloth. She watched with joy as the coffee grounds collected on the cloth and the brew soaked through.

The smell of the coffee tickled Elisabeth's nose. She had drunk coffee and milk for breakfast when she was perhaps Rosina's age, even dunking bread in it sometimes. In the evenings, Tata enjoyed a cup as he taught Elisabeth.

But the war had made the beans expensive, so for the past few years, all the Schuhmachers could offer their guests for hot drinks were teas made from plants in their garden, mostly peppermint and chamomile.

Stefan stood up, having finished smoothing out the dent in the floor.

"That was so kind of you. Thank you so much. How can I repay you?"

His eyes glowed with a little mischief. "Do I get to have the first cup of coffee?"

Elisabeth's heart leaped to her throat. He clearly meant that as more than a request.

Maybe Stefan would take coffee as my dowry payment. The idea was worth a thought.

She poured a cup and handed it to him. Stefan helped himself to the small pitcher of milk and a little sugar, took a sip, and smiled. "This tastes wonderful, Lissika. Thank you."

"They're here!" Rosina announced as she ran in the side door.

Elisabeth jumped again and prayed to Jesus to please ask people to stop startling her.

"They" were friends of Tata and their wives. The men walked around to the back of the house, since Tata was sitting outside. Several raised their eyebrows as they passed the side door, probably because Stefan was in the kitchen alone with Elisabeth and her best friend.

Their wives entered, looked Stefan up and down, and insisted on helping. Wanting to avoid being asked personal questions, Elisabeth suggested instead they take coffee and food to their husbands. "Maria and I will look after the rest. Mammi and Anna are also helping, but they're outside."

Several disapproving looks from the women told Elisabeth they understood her intent: to get them out of the kitchen, where Stefan...

Elisabeth glanced around. Where had he gone?

When the women left, Maria smiled. "He is a sly one," she said. "He snuck out while those women weren't watching."

Elisabeth had to laugh at his behaviour. For someone who was twenty-two years old, he sometimes acted like a boy. In a good way.

A little coffee left in the pot, she offered a half-filled cup to Maria, who declined.

"You deserve a break. I'll begin the next pot." She

winked at Elisabeth. "Besides, I believe someone will be dancing a lot with you this evening at the tavern."

Elisabeth couldn't wait. In her heart, she hoped that if Tata saw how nicely Stefan treated her at the community dance, and how much she enjoyed dancing with him, then he would welcome Stefan into their family.

She said a little prayer to Jesus for help.

The rest of the guests arrived shortly afterwards. Mammi and Anna carried food and drink outside, bringing plates and dishes inside as needed. Maria helped Elisabeth cut up more salami and cheese. All had agreed Rosina was too young to carry anything with so many people around.

By the time the passing around of food and drink had diminished, the dishes had become dangerously piled on one another.

Eva came in without her baby.

"Georg has Little Konrad right now," she said. She raised an eyebrow at the dirty dishes. "Looks like I arrived just in time."

Elisabeth grabbed both Eva's wrists and gave her a heartfelt thank you before stepping out to retrieve water from the well.

What she noticed gave her an uncomfortable sensation of nervousness and excitement: Stefan was tickling the baby in Georg's arms and making funny faces. He glanced up and waved to Elisabeth. She smiled back. He clearly wanted a family of his own and would enjoy being a father.

She returned with the water to find the dishes already piled and ready for washing: Eva and Maria had scraped many of them into the slop pail.

"Little Konrad was crying," Eva explained as Elisabeth poured the water into three basins. "Georg offered to take care of him for a little while. And Stefan, of course, can never stay away."

A husband who helped take care of his children. After what she had seen outside, Elisabeth was certain Stefan would do the same.

"But..." Maria paused, as though choosing her words carefully, "raising babies is women's work."

Elisabeth picked up the lump of homemade soap from the small table by the shelves and began scrubbing the first plate. "I think it's important for babies to feel the care and love of both parents. Why do men have to wait until their sons—if they have sons—are old enough to hold a hammer before they pay any attention to them?"

Maria seemed to think about what Elisabeth had said as she rinsed each plate twice: once to remove the rest of the soap, and once to give a final rinse. "I never thought of it that way." She turned to Eva. "Doesn't Frau Schuhmacher object to her son helping?"

Eva nodded. "Every day. She comments a lot on how shameful it is that he helps." Eva sighed. "I would do almost anything not to have to live with her." Eva dried the plate Maria handed her.

"That sounds very difficult," Maria said.

"It is. I must admit I regretted marrying Georg at first and was scared to be expecting a child. Some of his fits were about his first baby and wife. But ever since Little Konrad was born..." She peered out the window, where Georg and Stefan could be seen near the bird coops, still playing with Little Konrad. Her shoulders relaxed and a small expression of gratitude brightened her face. "He has been such a devoted father. He takes our baby at night after I've fed him so the rest of us can get some sleep. Georg works during the day, but once he's cleaned up, he looks after our son so I can work faster in the kitchen."

Elisabeth continued listening as Eva described all the ways that Georg helped with their baby. Although Little Konrad was too young to eat solid food—Eva still needed to feed him—Georg happily carried him around their property any time he could.

Would Stefan do the same? Judging by what Elisabeth had witnessed, yes.

"Stefan will treat you like a rose, Lissika," Maria said.

"The two of you would be perfect together," Eva added. "To see the changes in Georg since Christmas, all because you helped me understand what his life had been like on the front, means you'll be a very special wife to Stefan."

The dirty plate pile finally seemed smaller. Elisabeth would soon need to fetch more water, since the water in her basin was becoming too dirty.

"I don't know if Tata sees that." She explained to Eva what she had already shared with Maria, and Eva shook her head at her description of Tata's lack of interest in Stefan.

"If anyone leads a life different from what the community believes they should be leading," Eva said, "which Georg and I must do because of his fits—they find fault with it, though I don't know why. How does Georg spending time with his baby son change their lives at all? It makes him better. I'm certain he's had fewer fits since Little Konrad was born."

The three young women washed in silence for a few minutes, the question hanging in the air.

"We all dress the same," Elisabeth said. "I wonder if many people simply find comfort in things that are the same?"

"You might be right," Maria said. "I still get stares at my bangs."

"I think I do, too."

Eva laughed. "Then maybe I should join you. Just to bother people even more."

"I can cut your hair!" Maria offered.

Eva declined, but Elisabeth liked the idea of the three of them having the same haircut.

Elisabeth excused herself to get fresh water for her basin. As she opened the door and stepped outside, several women entered, hoping for more food.

Elisabeth helped serve them, but no sooner had she begun than she understood their real reason for coming inside.

"I don't know how you allow your husband to carry your baby," one said to Eva.

Eva's grip on the cutlery she was drying tightened. "He cares for our baby as much as I do. That's enough of a reason."

The other woman snickered. "Wait a little, and he'll soon be helping with the dishes."

Elisabeth prayed to Jesus for patience so she didn't "accidentally" dump her dirty water on these women.

"You wouldn't want help with the dishes?" Elisabeth asked them.

The first woman scoffed. "Of course. But I would never ask my husband to help. That's what daughters are for."

They thanked Elisabeth for the food and coffee and left.

Maria's eyes were wide as she stared at the door closing behind them. "I know so many in our church can be rude, but that was too harsh."

Eva took a deep breath. "I deal with that almost every day." She looked up. "But I would never ever want a husband other than Georg. His days at war have turned him into this...this peaceful giant who does his best to see the good in others."

Elisabeth mulled over Eva's words as she fetched more

water. She remembered Eva from before Christmas: she had belittled others, gossiped, and otherwise behaved like many of the women in their congregation. Elisabeth actually hadn't liked her then. But the more she got to know her, the more she realized that Eva was just trying to survive in a household full of mean people. Eva had since learned to stand her ground when it came to Georg, and now Little Konrad.

Elisabeth returned with the water, and Eva nudged her down the line. "You've washed so many dishes, your skin will fall off. It's my turn." Elisabeth didn't object. The soap had indeed dried out her hands. Rinsing and drying would be a welcome break.

"I'm worried that your father will offer someone else your hand," Maria said.

"I am, too. I would like to..." She had never said this desire out loud. "I would like to marry Stefan." Elisabeth blinked back tears.

Maria stood up straight and held out her hand like a man to Eva. "Let's promise right here and now that we will help Elisabeth marry the man she wants."

Eva's face turned playfully stern, and she shook Maria's hand.

All the women laughed, and Elisabeth couldn't be more thankful for her friends.

CHAPTER THIRTEEN

Juliana jumped up and down in the studio, her tap shoes clattering on the floor, and patted her best friend on the shoulder. "Our first time dancing together since Christmas!"

Rachel laughed. "You have not changed."

Jasmine, her arms crossed, said, "You're wasting the energy you could be using on dance."

Juliana understood it was not a true criticism but more an observation. Jasmine could come across as very direct, and since she was hyper-focused on her dance career, somewhat snobby. But Juliana had learned to accept her as she was, and Jasmine had become a good friend who also helped Juliana improve her technique.

"I have to let my energy out somehow, and Miss Denise isn't here yet."

Jasmine shook her head in resignation.

Mrs. Laing, the office administrator, entered the studio with someone following her. It was Austin! Juliana's pulse skyrocketed. Why was he here? Austin only danced ballet.

Jasmine's eyes opened wide, and a true—and sadly rare—grin appeared on her face. "Hey, Austin!" she called out.

Some in the class giggled. Juliana had no idea what that was about.

Austin waved back.

Mackenzie leaned over to Juliana. "Jasmine had the biggest crush on Austin when she was twelve or thirteen, before she knew he was gay."

Juliana covered her face as she smiled, but Jasmine had apparently overheard.

"Makes sense to get together with a guy who loves ballet. Then we could practise together," she declared.

Juliana tried hard not to giggle. "You have your life planned out this much?"

Jasmine's face made it look like it was obvious that you should plan every aspect of your career as soon as possible.

I wish, Juliana thought. But with Rachel and Sophie's encouragement, she had typed up a bunch of her essay last night after her talk with Pauline. This afternoon, she'd spoken with Mr. Casimiro. Just one more person to find.

Mrs. Laing called everyone's attention and introduced Austin, her kind smile calming Juliana's nervousness and excitement. "Miss Denise had to leave. She's been dealing with a headache all day and realized that ninety minutes of tap class wouldn't help."

Laughter filled the room. Everyone could relate.

"Hey." Austin waved. "Miss Denise asked me to pick a piece of music for you and turn this evening into a choreo class. You can work in whatever groups you want to create something."

Everyone cheered.

"The three of us?" Juliana asked Jasmine and Rachel, and they agreed.

"Let's take ten minutes to warm up," Austin said, "and I'll find the music. Miss Denise said to make it something you've probably never danced to before."

What did that mean? But before Juliana could even think of an answer, the room filled with the cacophony of twenty or so dancers—forty or so tap shoes—tapping, striking, scraping, and pounding the floor. Although a coordinated warm-up session would've ensured everyone tapped in unison with the music, even then it still would've been loud.

It was no wonder Miss Denise went home to nurse her headache.

After ten minutes were up, Austin asked everyone to quiet down.

"This piece is by a composer named Ludovico Einaudi. The title translates into 'White Cloud.' That may mean something to you, or it may not. It certainly doesn't have to.

But before you begin, I'd like you to first think of how the music makes you feel. Less about how it makes your feet feel. More about how it makes your heart feel."

Juliana shot Rachel and Jasmine a confused look. Rachel mirrored it, but Jasmine seemed enamoured by everything Austin said.

Austin hit play, and within eight counts, Juliana wanted to begin tapping. *So that's what he means*, she thought. *Wait and see what the music makes me feel before I start tapping.*

The song began with a progression of slow chords. Then it paused, and light notes from a piano filled the studio. The song continued, with high notes playing the melody and lower notes supporting it.

Despite the song's happy feel, anger began to fill Juliana's heart. Where was *that* coming from? The music sped up a little, but it continued to retain the high and low notes.

Then it stopped. Feet started moving until Austin reminded everyone to remain still. The music picked up again with its melody, but softer.

Something released in Juliana, a resolution of some kind.

But if she felt a resolution, what was the problem? What had caused her anger?

Austin turned off the music.

"In your groups, share your thoughts. And feelings." He glanced up at the clock high on the wall. "No taps for another five minutes. I'll play the music again as you discuss your impressions."

Jasmine got right to the point. "You're angry about something," she said to Juliana.

Juliana agreed, admitting she didn't know what she felt angry about.

"That's easy," Rachel said. "Your grandfather."

"Opa? But why...?"

Why would Juliana be angry with Opa? Frustrated by his Alzheimer's, sure. But that wasn't his fault. If anything, she felt sorry for him and did her best to help.

Angry...

Some of his old-fashioned opinions? Again, they annoyed Juliana and sometimes surprised her because he was otherwise so kind. To hear how he used to treat his son for being gay had hurt Juliana. But to see him now fully support Uncle Peter and his engagement to Brian brought Juliana nothing but joy. And sure, Opa still made comments about women being better suited for the kitchen, but comments like those felt more like observations to Juliana, not statements of how the world should work.

Angry...

Juliana couldn't think of anything.

Then it hit her. "I'm not angry *at* him. I'm angry with my parents for not making sure I got to know him sooner."

Then came the release Juliana had felt in the music.

Was it truly possible that music could awaken emotions and thoughts Juliana wasn't conscious of?

Jasmine raised an eyebrow. "That's interesting, actually. The music sounds happy to me. Like it's full of possibilities. What makes you hear anger?"

Juliana explained how the notes and the quality of the playing made her feel like she deserved a happy, worry-free relationship with her grandfather, one where she had known him before his Alzheimer's began developing.

"Ah, I see. You hear the happiness, but you feel like you don't get to have any of it."

Juliana nodded. "That's it exactly."

Rachel sniffled.

"You okay?" Juliana asked.

"What you just said made me think of how important that photo of your grandfather's mother was to him. I have so many photos of my mom, which I'll forever be grateful for. But to see him so panicked about losing one... My heart breaks for him that all he has left of her is a few photos and her book of drawings." She tried to dry her eyes, but tears kept falling. "I'm scared that I'll be mourning Mom's death the rest of my life. Like...these horrible feelings will never end." She wiped her eyes again, and Juliana put an arm around her.

Austin came over with a tissue box. "Everything okay? Can I help somehow?"

Rachel gratefully accepted a tissue. "I'll be fine. I just didn't know...that I was scared of something."

Austin tilted his head to the side. "That doesn't sound good."

Rachel blew her nose and tried to swallow back her tears.

Juliana stepped in. "Her mom was killed by a drunk driver earlier this year."

Austin's eyes grew wide. "I'm sorry. I thought the song sounded hopeful. I'm really sorry. Maybe I should change the music."

Jasmine had an expression of sympathy on her face. "My dad's a police officer," she said. "And Mom's an ER nurse. I've heard too many stories like that."

Austin scratched the back of his neck. He clearly felt uncomfortable. Juliana had to clear the air a little and take the attention off Rachel.

"So, how are we supposed to choreograph to this?" she asked. "I feel anger. Rachel, sadness. And Jasmine..." She looked toward her new friend. "Happiness?"

Jasmine shrugged, suddenly not as confident as she usually was. "I hope that's not insensitive. But I do see so many ways life can play out in the music. Maybe some of them are sad, but many of them are happy."

"You see hope," Austin said.

Hope.

Can I see the possibilities that still exist for Opa? For how I can help him? Maybe eventually help others?

The music paused at that moment. "That's what I felt!" Juliana exclaimed. "That's the resolution."

"Can you explain that to me?" Austin asked.

Juliana tried, but she kept stumbling on her words. How did acknowledging her anger at her parents cause that release, that feeling that everything would be okay?

Austin laughed kindly. "I think you've found your feelings."

"But how do we combine all this?" Jasmine asked. "The three of us are basically hearing different music."

Austin shaped his hands as though he were holding something round. "When it comes right down to it, emotions are a revolving ball: all the same object, just different sides. It took me a while to figure that out, but once I did, I found it easier to dance."

"Because dance doesn't get caught up in words," Jasmine said.

"Exactly," Austin replied.

"Um...?" Rachel held up her tissues, a tiny questioning smile on her face. Juliana pointed to the waste bin.

"Is she going to be okay?" Austin asked, watching Rachel as she threw out her tissues.

"She's been through so much," Juliana said, "but dance has kept her going."

Austin pressed his lips together and stared at the floor for a moment. "I know the feeling."

When Rachel returned, Austin moved on to the next group.

The girls spent the next forty-five minutes choreographing their combination, paying attention to how they felt as the music played. Juliana's anger was funnelled into loud sounds; Jasmine's happiness into quick, light sounds; and Rachel's sadness about her family into drawn-out sounds.

With a half-hour left in the class, everyone sat down at the front, and each group of two to four dancers showed their choreography.

Juliana laughed at some of them—the ones who saw humour in the music—and cried with others. One piece of music, so many interpretations.

So many possibilities.

"Juliana, Jasmine, and Rachel?"

The girls squeezed each other's hands and walked to the centre of the studio.

Austin hit play, and within moments, their different emotions expressed themselves through the percussion of tap. But now that they were the only three dancing, the sounds reached Juliana's ears with a new intensity. The anger shot out through her feet, while the pitter-patter of Jasmine's taps sounded almost like laughter. Rachel's scrapes and occasional fast movements in her feet sounded like moans and sniffles.

The three continued, not forgetting once any of the steps they had memorized in a short time. When they finished and Austin stopped the music, the room remained silent for a few moments.

Rachel broke out into tears. Juliana hugged her tight, and Jasmine, too. Before Juliana knew what was happening, the sounds of dozens of taps on the floor told her the class was walking toward them, and a group hug followed, with Rachel at the centre.

This is what dance is about, Juliana thought. No one said a word: they just moved to express their support.

Not only would Juliana find a way to keep dancing—she could feel her conviction in her bones—but she would also find a way to keep making happy memories with Opa.

CHAPTER FOURTEEN

The accordion, clarinet, and trumpet brought the entire tavern to its feet.

Or so it felt to Elisabeth, who was standing at the back against the wall, watching her friends dance to their heart's content, while the older members of their church remained seated, rarely taking their eyes off the dance floor as they chattered with one another. Occasionally, someone threw a glance in Elisabeth's direction and then leaned over to their neighbour to whisper something.

No one had asked Elisabeth to dance—she assumed it was because *everyone else* assumed she and Stefan would soon make a formal announcement. But Stefan wouldn't ask her either, and Elisabeth didn't blame him: her father kept his intimidating eye on him and Georg—standing on the other side of the room against the wall—the entire time.

Georg stands there because he doesn't like crowds, she thought. *I'm standing here to avoid listening to my family gossip about me.*

She stared down at her blue-green cashmere skirt, the one Omama had made her for her first dance after her confirmation. Elisabeth's grandmother had also colourfully embroidered the thin white-cotton blouse she now wore, including adding the red ribbons along the sleeves. She adjusted her shawl—white fabric with orange, red, blue-green, and yellow flowers sewn into it—which flowed over her shoulders and crossed over her chest, by tucking the ends again into her skirt. Despite how much care she'd taken to look attractive, she might as well have dressed for an ordinary day on the *salasch*. She was thoroughly exhausted from Tata's welcome-home celebration. Why had she taken all this time to prepare for an evening of fun and dancing when no one would dance with her?

When the jovial polka ended, the band announced a break, and Maria and Hagel Konrad left the dance floor. Hagel Konrad returned to his parents' table, and Maria to hers. Elisabeth joined her, relieved to have a little distraction.

"You look like you're having so much fun!" She hoped she came across as excited and not bored.

Maria gulped down her coffee, which must've been

lukewarm at best. "Konrad can dance so well," she said. "He's hard to keep up with."

"Given that you've singed your hair on the oven, almost gotten run over by a bicycle, and fallen through ice...I'd say you're doing quite well."

Maria shot Elisabeth a playful look, then bade Elisabeth go with her to the bar. After treating Elisabeth to a coffee, Maria led them outside for fresh air. The sun had just begun to set, and the cooler evening air refreshed Elisabeth, giving her hope that Tata might still change his mind.

"I hope I'll make Konrad happy," Maria confessed.

"What in heaven's name would make you say that?"

Maria blew at her cup. "He gets angry quickly. I'm sure I just need to pay better attention to what he likes. People can change, after all."

So Elisabeth had been right to refuse him in the winter as a husband. But she also didn't want her best friend to end up with such a man. Could this marriage be stopped? "What does your mother say about it?"

"She said there was nothing wrong with that and to learn as fast as I can what he likes and doesn't like."

Elisabeth's throat closed. Of course there was something wrong with that. Didn't Jesus say to love thy neighbour as thyself? Why did so many in their church believe it didn't apply to family?

"I see." What else was there to say? Maria was engaged.

She couldn't pull out now: it would shame her family for years, maybe even generations. Deaf Lissi had gotten her name from an ancestor who had been deaf, even though she herself could hear just fine. Maria's new nickname could become Runaway Maria. What would her grandchildren think about that? Assuming she had any, since no man would marry a woman who'd ended her first engagement.

I warned her about him, she thought. *Why didn't she listen?*

But Elisabeth had also only been fourteen when she'd warned Maria about Hagel Konrad. What did a fourteen-year-old know about marriage? *But does being fifteen suddenly mean I know a lot?* The answer was no.

"Have you tried talking to him?" she asked.

Maria nodded. "He said it's my duty to make him happy." She sipped from her coffee. "So, I'll keep trying."

"What about praying?" In Elisabeth's experience, Jesus and God didn't speak to her. But maybe they spoke to others.

Maria nodded again. "Nothing's changed."

"I'm sorry." The usual words of comfort would've been something like *We don't always understand why God gives us these challenges.* But if people were supposed to love each other as they did themselves, and Jesus loved all, then why didn't God help? God had protected Mammi, who could've died when her body no longer could carry the baby. He had brought Tata home safe and sound—even if Tata had changed. Their crops this year were growing well.

Did God make some people go through really hard times and give others an easier life? Or maybe God just couldn't pay attention to so many people at once, and when He did something nice for someone, something bad happened for others.

But then how did that explain the war?

Or what if what evil people pray for isn't what God wants them to have, and then they get angry and become mean to others? she thought. *Maybe they ask for land or money, and when God doesn't give it to them, they start fights. And emperors start wars.* That made more sense.

"Lissika?" Maria pulled Elisabeth out of her thoughts. "You look like you're far away."

Elisabeth took a sip of her coffee. "Just thinking about nonsense." Not wanting to give away what she'd actually been thinking, Elisabeth offered the first idea that came to her to help her best friend: "How about you invite me over a lot when you're married? I can help with the baking, and we can have lots of nice talks together."

Maria smiled. "You are really kind, Lissika. I would like that."

Was that God speaking through Elisabeth? She didn't feel any different, but where had that idea come from?

They continued drinking their coffees.

"How are things going with Stefan?"

Elisabeth shrugged. "He hasn't asked me to dance at all this evening. I'm certain some of the older ladies are staring at me now, wondering what's happened."

"He's probably scared to ask you because he knows what your father thinks."

Elisabeth sighed. "Tata's been staring at him the whole time, and not in a friendly way."

Maria straightened herself and faced Elisabeth square on. "You have to do something about it, Lissika. Convince your father."

Shivers ran down Elisabeth's body. Stand up to Tata? She'd missed him so terribly since he'd left last November. If she stood up to him, he'd think she hated him. It was a daughter's job to be obedient.

Maria drank her last bit of coffee, peered into Elisabeth's cup, and, seeing it was empty, grabbed Elisabeth by the hand. "You're done, too. Let's go." Before Elisabeth could ask what Maria was doing, she was pulled back into the tavern. The band was just taking up their instruments again. Maria dragged Elisabeth across the dance floor to her family's table.

The tavern fell silent. Did people really care *this much* about who Elisabeth married?

She didn't need anyone to answer that question.

Maria placed their cups onto the table, almost dropping them. She snatched up Elisabeth's white handkerchief that she would need for dancing, stuffed it into her hand, dragged her across the dance floor again, and moments later led Elisabeth to stand in front of Stefan.

"This is what friends do," Maria declared and disappeared as quickly as she'd pulled Elisabeth into this awkward moment.

Thankfully, the band started playing.

Elisabeth's cheeks heated up as Stefan's bemused face seemed to ask what this was about, while Georg's smile showed he knew.

Elisabeth stared at the floor. Women didn't ask men to dance. He'd certainly avoid her from this moment on if she asked him.

"Ask her finally." Georg gently nudged his best friend. To Elisabeth, he said, "He's boring tonight, anyway."

Ask her finally? Did that mean Stefan had been wanting to ask Elisabeth to dance the entire time? Her heart fluttered.

Stefan shook his head as he laughed. "Sometimes, Georg, you surprise me." He held out his left arm for Elisabeth. "Would you join me?"

Elisabeth forced her feet to stay planted to the ground so she wouldn't jump up and down like an excited child. "Yes, I would." She placed her hand on his arm, a warm sensation rushing through her body.

Her white handkerchief in hand, she and Stefan took

up the customary position on the dance floor and jumped right into the polka. Elisabeth's heart sang with joy. Stefan would protect her, help her, stay loyal to her.

But as Stefan spun her around, Elisabeth caught a look of anger in her father's eye. Her throat tightened.

Maybe this hadn't been such a good idea after all.

CHAPTER FIFTEEN

The girls dropped their dance bags on the floor and plopped onto Juliana's bed.

"You must be exhausted," Rachel said. "You're not even opening your bag and sprinkling baking soda in your shoes."

"I feel like I've been hit by a bus. I always thought I put emotion into my dance. But tonight...? Tonight felt different. Deeper. Like, from a part I didn't know I had."

Rachel nodded.

Juliana's memories travelled back to her last dance at their studio in Calgary before she moved. The intense anger of the impending move had coursed through her body and burst out of her. And how often had she banged out her frustrations here, on her tap board? The music in class tonight, though oddly happy-sounding, had brought out her anger again. But when she talked about it with Jasmine and Rachel, Juliana realized she was angry because she was sad. Hurt.

"Hey, Rach?"

"Yeah?"

"Do you think anger isn't really an emotion?"

Rachel sat up. "That's the weirdest thing I think you've ever asked me."

Juliana continued to stare at the ceiling. "Like...maybe it is an emotion, but not a real one."

"If it's not a real emotion, then it's a fake one?"

Rachel had a good point. What was Juliana trying to say? She grabbed Elisabeth's book of drawings and opened it to the one of the lantern.

Rachel gently turned the book toward herself and studied it for a moment. "It's beautiful. So much life in how she drew those flames."

Juliana turned the book back around. "I showed this to Jasmine a while back. When your mom died, actually."

"Really?"

"Yeah. Jasmine said my dancing that night had changed. Improved in a way other than technique. Like I was expressing something important."

Tears began to well up in Rachel's eyes. "That makes me so happy, Jules. To know that Mom's passing had something good attached to it."

"Oh my god, Rach! I didn't mean to suggest that something good—"

Rachel interrupted. "That's not what I meant all." She placed the book on her lap, her fingers passing above the page so as not to smudge the drawing. "I don't know who—or what—decides when we die. Or if anything does. Maybe Mom was supposed to die like that from the moment she was born. I'm not sure I believe in fate, but I'll never know. I just mean that to know that something good came of it makes the pain a little easier to bear."

Juliana had no response to that. How could she say anything without making it sound she was glad Kim had died?

"Don't do that to me," Rachel said.

"Do what?"

"Treat me differently, as though we can't talk about Mom."

"Um...I..." Juliana just wanted to be respectful of Rachel's feelings. She hadn't realized she was hurting Rachel. But she still didn't understand how.

Rachel's voice became quiet. "I need to share something with you. Something that just felt weird to talk about during our calls."

Juliana braced herself. Had she misread something? What couldn't Rachel share?

"I can't cry like that in front of our friends back home." Rachel bit her lip as she thought. Juliana did her best to let

Rachel take her time. Only after a long pause did Rachel continue. "When Mom died, I felt new expectations on me. Don't get me wrong—everyone was helpful, asking if they could do something for me, or if I needed to talk. But they wouldn't let me be me plus this horrible loss. I could only be the loss."

Juliana's stomach churned. She had thought everything was going relatively well back home. What had she misread? She hadn't expected Rachel to "just get over" her mother's death. But she'd never thought about this side of grief, about the expectations others might have of the person grieving.

"I'm sorry if—"

Rachel stared at the duvet and shook her head. "Let me finish."

Juliana swallowed. "Sorry."

"What I mean is that I see life so differently now. Before Mom died, if I ever read about a death online or some local murder story from the newspaper, I didn't think much of it. But now when I catch a headline like that, I think, 'Was that person a father? Brother? Sister? What hole have they left behind?'" She rubbed her hands on her thighs. "Even when Jasmine said what her parents do and what they've told her, I couldn't help wonder who they were talking about."

Her hands froze for a moment, and Juliana wondered if she should say anything. Would Rachel judge her silence to mean Juliana didn't want to talk about Kim? Or did Rachel just need time to collect her thoughts?

Rachel folded her hands together and continued. "Dance fills that hole for me as much as it can. But if I start crying, everyone's on top of me to try and make me happy again. They won't let me just be sad for those two minutes. If I'm really happy—and that's been happening more and more recently—they still ask if I'm okay because they think I'm hiding something. It's like, on the one hand, they don't want me to be sad. On the other, they expect me to be sad all the time. I just can't." She wiped tears from her cheeks and grabbed a tissue from Juliana's nightstand. "The way your classmates just hugged me like that...no clown faces, no stupid jokes, nothing. Just...support. No wonder you chose this place."

Now Juliana understood. Rachel had interpreted Juliana's silence as Juliana refusing to accept Rachel seeing something positive coming from her mother's death. That positive moment had been a gift for Rachel, and Juliana had pushed it back.

"I chose this studio because of how everyone seemed to treat each other online. They were nice to each other, tagged each other in fun comments, and really supported each other. And there was Austin, who uses dance to fight against bullying, create awareness for epilepsy, and support anyone who wants to dance but is facing their own hurdles."

Rachel nodded. "So although some—like Jasmine and Austin—want to make a career out of dance, what pulled you to the studio is how happy everyone is there."

"And that they want to share that happiness." Juliana took a deep breath in as something inside her released. She sat up and pointed to the lantern. "Jasmine told me that my dancing that night had been like this flame—alive. I remember the feeling: The anger I had inside me because of your mom and because I couldn't be at her funeral with you shot through in streams throughout my body. And tonight... From working with you and Jasmine, I think I've realized that anger is a protector. It's trying to keep me from feeling my real feelings."

"It's trying to keep you from seeing whatever the flame in the lantern is actually trying to show you."

"Yes."

Juliana shivered as the truth of what she'd just said became real. She'd reacted in anger to this move because being torn away from her friends and the life she loved hurt too much.

She'd been angry at Dad after her first day of tap class when she'd forgotten her shoes because she'd been too embarrassed by her own mistake.

She'd been angry at how Kim had died and how Juliana couldn't be by Rachel's side to help because she'd felt completely lost about how to be a best friend from such a distance.

And now her anger was protecting her from feeling regret and sadness at what was happening to Opa.

But most of all, it was protecting her from feeling scared about Opa someday passing away and how soon that day might come.

"Pass me the tissues." Juliana pointed to the box, within Rachel's reach, as tears started streaming down her face.

"Anger tries to protect us from pain," she said in gulps.

Rachel grabbed a fistful of tissues, and she cried, too.

The girls hugged each other tight. As they cried, Juliana's body let go of the tension she'd unknowingly been holding on to all these months. Yes, some things had improved, but the pain from deep down, the pain about Opa that got unearthed tonight, that pain had never before had a moment to talk to her to let her know it existed. Now it had finally found its voice.

That's not completely true, she realized as she and Rachel separated. *That panic attack from the old age home was part of this. I just didn't recognize it or what it was saying.*

"Looks like we both got something unexpected out of tonight," Rachel said, her eyes finally dry, though still puffy. "But for me, it wasn't just about Mom. I think I know now what I want to do with my life."

Juliana threw the last of her tissues into the waste bin. "What's that?"

"I want to help other kids through really tough things like this. Maybe I'll become a therapist. Or maybe I'll teach.

I don't know if it would be in schools or at a dance studio. I mean, Austin's eighteen?" Juliana nodded in confirmation. "So, he hasn't been teaching for twenty years. But because of his hard times in life, he somehow managed to help us. So...maybe I do want to be a dance teacher? I can help kids connect their feelings with their bodies, and then they could love dance the way you and I do. I don't know... maybe?"

Juliana let out a cry of joy. "That would be so perfect for you!" She hugged Rachel tight. "I think you should do it. Give the apprenticeship program at home your all and see what happens."

Rachel drew in a deep breath and let it out. "My god, that feels so good. And so right. After Mom's death, my life was full of unknowns: learning how to live with Dad, figuring out that I had to cook by myself if I didn't want another frozen meal, helping Dad move back to within my high school's boundaries so I wouldn't lose my friends at school on top of everything. It left me so much in limbo."

That all made sense to Juliana, and she couldn't be happier for Rachel. She squealed as she clapped her hands and bounced on her bed. Rachel laughed at the sight.

CHAPTER SIXTEEN

Tata helped Elisabeth adjust the leather straps attached to a basket that now hung on her back. There were many chores she didn't like: cleaning the floors Saturday mornings, shovelling the compost pile from their home onto the wagon, and whitewashing the walls every spring. She did them, of course, because being punished was worse, but she truly disliked them.

Moving up and down the *salasch* fields with a basket on her back, the straps digging into her shoulders, was perhaps the worst of them all. To spend the day out in the glaring late-summer sun, her back feeling only pain by the end of the day, always made the following day impossible for her.

Not that Mammi or Tata cared: they said you just had to continue.

"You can stay inside and help Deaf Lissi," Stefan offered. "Georg, Samuel, and I can pull the extra leaves and baby ears off the corn." He lifted the basket and threaded his stump into one strap before leaning sideways as he pushed his full arm into the other. Georg helped him adjust it.

Staying inside in this heat, helping with cleaning or chopping vegetables, sounded much more inviting to Elisabeth, especially because Deaf Lissi was expecting a baby, too. After what had happened to Mammi, Elisabeth believed that helping Deaf Lissi spend more time sitting instead of running her household would improve the chances of the baby being born.

"Lissika can help on our *salasch*," Tata said firmly. "Luki has to help me repair some tools, and the other two are in town, helping Lissa with preserving."

Elisabeth gave Stefan a thankful look, which she hoped Tata didn't catch.

"Where is he?" Georg asked.

"Who?" Tata replied. "Everyone's here."

But the glazed look in Georg's eyes told Elisabeth he was losing himself in a nightmare of a fit. "Georg, is everything all right?"

He shook his head. "I have to find him."

At least he can hear me, she thought.

Stefan placed a calm hand on Georg's shoulder, and Georg didn't fight back. That probably meant he wasn't seeing a fight or in some way fearing for his life. Otherwise, he would've believed Stefan to be one of the attackers and pushed him away.

"Lissa will never forgive me if I don't bring him home."

Tata sighed, shook his head, and bade Luki follow him to the shed.

Elisabeth stared after Tata, shocked by his coldness. Where was the compassionate father she had known before Christmas? Her father certainly didn't hold back discipline when it was called for, but he never said no to a request for help, even offering to repair or make shoes when someone couldn't pay him right away. He always said they'd pay him eventually, and so far as Elisabeth knew, they had.

Seeing that Stefan and Samuel were helping Georg, Elisabeth shook the basket off her back and followed her father and brother to the shed.

"How can you leave your nephew like that?"

Tata turned around. "He's hardly a child, Lissika."

"He's still family. You know he's troubled. Just because you don't have nightmares from repairing dead men's boots doesn't mean you can treat him like that."

"Dead men's boots?" Luki asked, his eyes wide open.

Tata picked up a sheet of sandpaper and gave it to Luki. "Take those two hammers over there outside and rub this paper up and down the handles until they're smooth."

"What dead men's boots?" Luki asked.

"Nothing for your ears. Now, go." Tata held his hand behind Luki's bottom, and Luki ran out before Tata could give him a light tap.

Tata rubbed his hand over his face. "Where did you learn that? That is not for your ears—or your mind."

"Why do you protect me like this?" Elisabeth asked. "You taught me to learn, how to ask questions, how to read. But now? You don't want me to know certain things. Why?"

Tata sat down on a bench. "We don't have time for this."

"I do. I need to know. You've changed so much that the man I want to marry is scared to ask you for my hand because he sees how you look at him. So do I." She crossed her arms. "I need to know why you've changed."

Tata didn't answer immediately, and Elisabeth worried she'd angered him. But how else was she going to get an answer if she didn't speak her mind? Maybe women were supposed to stay silent in church like the Bible said, but it didn't command women—so far as she knew—to stay silent in a shed.

"I've changed because the world is changing," Tata said. "That encyclopedia is decades old. The knowledge it has is old. You've lived a protected life here in Semlak. It needs to stay that way."

Elisabeth couldn't believe what she was hearing. "Protected life? Mammi losing a baby is a protected life? Is helping Georg understand his nightmares? Dealing with Mammi's anger because of the baby and your leaving?

Helping Anna heal her ankle? Being the only confirmand in my class whose father *chose* to leave? How is any of that protected? If anything, the more I read, the more I learned, and the more I could help others." Realizing she'd been shouting, she lowered her voice. "And the more I could find help for myself in the Bible and Luther's words. You taught me that." Tears welled up in her eyes. "Because whenever I tried to talk to another adult besides you, I was yelled at, sometimes even ridiculed, for trying to learn how to be compassionate when people like Pastor Fröhlich, Konrad-Bátschi, and Margarethe-Néni were so cruel to Georg."

Tata patted a spot on the bench next to him, and she sat down. He said nothing for a time, his long breaths suggesting he was deep in thought.

Would he now forbid her from ever marrying Stefan? Had she acted so rudely that he would never grant her another wish in her life?

But she kept Eva and Maria's words in her heart: they would do whatever they could to help her and Stefan marry. Elisabeth needed to do that, too.

Tata set his straw hat down on his other side. "I wish you hadn't said that in front of Luki. How much more does he know?"

"Very little, if anything. He knows things scare Georg and that's why he has those nightmares when he's awake. But Luki looks up to him. Georg showed him how to use a hammer and to repair a fence. Tata, he was so proud when he learned to use a hammer."

Tata nodded, taking in what she said. His shoulders drooped, and he wrung his hands. "Someone like Georg can become dangerous, Lissika."

Did her father really think she didn't know this? "Tata, Stefan has gotten bruised from trying to help him. I know. That Stefan stays by Georg's side despite his troubles shows how compassionate and caring he is."

"He can't make money that way. The world is changing. You need someone who can take care of you."

Elisabeth stood up, her hands clenched into fists. How could her father speak like that, given everything that had happened while he was away?

"You left me alone for almost an entire year. All I ask is to be allowed to marry a man who makes me happy and will care for me and my family with all his heart. You haven't even asked to see the drawings you wanted me to make for you. What am I supposed to think of that?"

She ran out of the workshop, tears flowing down her cheeks, only to run into Luki, who was sitting on the ground, sanding away at one hammer's handle.

"Lissika? Are you all right?"

Elisabeth tried her best to not sound like she was crying. "You can go back to Tata now. He wants you." She didn't know if Tata wanted him, but Luki would keep Tata busy.

She continued running toward the *salasch* house and leaned against a wall where she hoped no one would see her. If she took the wagon home, which she could most certainly do herself, she would anger her father even more. And then what? Where would she go besides her family's house? With all of them sleeping in the front room at night, Elisabeth couldn't have time to herself to ask God why everything had turned out this way.

She had tried so hard to be a good Christian, to take care of people who needed it, to support her family wherever she could, and yet, she couldn't have the future she wanted.

She slowly slid down the side of the white house and wrapped her arms around her knees. It was still early in the morning and just over four kilometres back to town. She could walk.

But with the sun beating down, she would become thirsty fast, and a woman didn't stop by the tavern outside of town—or any tavern for that matter—for a glass of water.

How could she feel surrounded by family and stranded at the same time?

A hand touched her shoulder. She looked up. It was Stefan. She jumped up and immediately tried to dry her eyes.

"I...I'm sorry. I was...my eyes are just...I was rubbing them..." Stefan would definitely not want a woman who couldn't hold herself together like Mammi could. Maybe Mammi got angry too often, but she didn't cry in front of people other than Tata when he arrived home. She probably cried in a room by herself after losing her baby, and maybe when Tata first left.

But that was it.

Elisabeth kept wiping her eyes until Stefan touched one of her hands to stop her.

"Luki said you were crying, and he ran to get me. Thankfully, we hadn't gone too far because of Georg's fit."

"Is he...?" Elisabeth had forgotten about her cousin. Could anything else go wrong?

"He's fine now. A little embarrassed, as he always is, but he's fine."

At least one good thing had happened today. In a way.

"May I?" Stefan opened his arms, inviting Elisabeth into an embrace. "You look like you need a friend."

If Tata saw her in Stefan's arms, he would most definitely tell everyone that Stefan was not a good man for her, and she would get a tongue lashing and a long time kneeling in dried corn kernels.

But she was so tired, so ready to give up on her future, that she didn't care what anyone thought. She leaned into him, and he wrapped his one arm lovingly around her.

"I know I can't provide for you the same way someone like Hagel Konrad can. But I will try my hardest to give you the best family I can."

Elisabeth pulled back, and Stefan pulled his handkerchief from his pocket and offered it to her. "I've stayed back," he said, "out of respect for your father's return. I remember how surprised I was when I returned: people had grown older, some had married, some had had children. Some had died. Your father returned to a town where his brother no longer lived."

Elisabeth felt guilty for being so angry at Tata and too focused on her own needs.

But could she be blamed? He held her happiness in his hands.

She took in a deep breath, finally ready to speak. "Thank you for your kindness." She passed back the handkerchief. She needed to tell Stefan something, so that he understood her intentions. "I like you because you help me see the world in a different way."

Delight shone through Stefan's eyes. "That makes me very happy."

He insisted she go inside to Deaf Lissi for something to eat and drink before joining the others in the fields.

Not wanting to anger Tata further, she fulfilled her duties on the *salasch* and was relieved as Tata taught Luki how to drive the wagon.

She waved to Georg, Deaf Lissi, and Stefan as they pulled out onto the road. Stefan doffed his straw hat and winked at her.

She smiled back at him.

Georg elbowed his friend, and Stefan returned the favour, followed by Samuel grabbing Stefan's hat off his head so Georg could mess up Stefan's hair. Stefan jumped away from both and ran his hand through his hair quickly, trying to neaten it up, before waving again to Elisabeth.

She laughed at their playfulness. Seeing Georg have fun like this warmed her heart and even eased her own pain a little. Becoming a father again had helped him heal some more.

God certainly worked in mysterious ways.

As the horse trotted down the long road back into town, Elisabeth tried to think of a way to convince her father once and for all that she deserved to marry Stefan.

Once home, everyone freshened up for a big supper outside that Mammi, Anna, and Rosina had prepared: a fresh salad, pork hocks, and boiled potatoes. Elisabeth ate as much as Tata did.

Finally feeling more like herself, she asked her father in front of the family: "Tata, what does Luther say about the role of the husband?"

"Why are you asking me? Didn't you study well enough for your confirmation?"

"I'd like to know if you remember."

Her siblings froze, staring at her with wide eyes. Mammi's face remained stern, but she didn't say anything. Would she explode at Elisabeth?

Or had something changed?

After Tata refused to answer, Elisabeth said, "Husbands are supposed to be considerate to their wives. They are to treat them with respect, because women are the weaker partner. Husbands are also not to be harsh with their wives."

Tata filled his mouth with food and chewed. When he finally finished, he sat up straight and banged his forefinger on the table. "Do you mean to say that I do not treat your mother *with respect*?"

Jesus, please help me stay calm. She continued speaking about Luther. "A wife's role is to submit to her husband. I will do so willingly to my husband, but only to a man I can respect. Furthermore, Luther says that fathers are not to exasperate their children. Instead, they must bring them up in the training and instruction of the Lord." Tata opened his mouth to speak, but Elisabeth had one more point to make. "And Jesus says to treat your neighbour as you would treat yourself. Therefore, the only man I should be allowed to marry is Stefan: he meets all of Luther's requirements for a proper Christian family man."

Tata wiped his mouth and drank his schnapps.

"Lukas," Mammi said. "She is right."

CHAPTER SEVENTEEN

By the end of the following day, Juliana had notes from her final interview in hand: Austin's mom, who used to work as an executive assistant but now ran the Belmont Village Chocolate Shop.

Which had a *brownie bar*! How had Juliana not known this? Who would keep such a delectable secret from her?

It was Saturday, the day Rachel would fly back to Calgary. Juliana, Rachel, and Sophie all wanted to enjoy something new.

"Serves you right for sticking too much to what's comfortable," Rachel said as she dug into her brownie-in-a-mug, topped with fresh strawberries and whipped cream.

Juliana couldn't argue: in part, because her mouth was full with brownie and chocolate syrup, and in part, because her best friend had spoken the truth. When

Juliana found something she loved, she rarely strayed from it.

Tracy, Austin's mom, came by, a grin on her face. "Looks like you three are enjoying your brownies."

Juliana had already stuffed her mouth with another spoonful, so all she could do was nod while the others expressed their gratitude for the free brownies.

Tracy smiled. "Anything for teens trying to figure out their lives. I know a thing or two about that."

She left them to their chocolate heaven.

But they weren't at the chocolate shop just for the brownies. They also wanted some comfort: Dad had taken them to the cemetery to see Georg's grave.

"Seeing that flat stone in the ground made everything so real to me," Rachel said. "With everything your family went through... And they weren't the only ones."

"And there are probably lots of people today whose lives are like that."

They ate in silence, conscious that it was almost time for Rachel to leave.

"If there's one thing I've come to accept," Rachel said, "it's that, even though we're far away from each other, we kind of aren't."

"But still, it's expensive to visit you," Juliana said, "and I've learned this past week that seeing you in person is so much better than over video calls."

No one said anything for a few minutes when Sophie

sat up straight. "We could all move in together! You two just have to study at the same university, and I'll move in with you, because I'm sure my family will be driving me nuts by then!"

Everyone laughed and high-fived each other, agreeing to try and figure out their futures in the next four or five years.

"But Elisabeth's life..." Juliana said. "I can't imagine."

"Your grandfather always did say it was hard."

"I just didn't know what that meant."

"Me neither," Sophie said. "To have lost her first husband to bullies... How horrible did they have to be that he...that he died?"

Rachel shook her head in amazement. "It really makes you wonder how the world turns if humans are capable of so much harm."

Sophie sipped on her pop. "That reminds me. With all this talk about our ancestors and your careers paper, Juliana, it got me thinking about my own future."

"Oh?"

Sophie pulled out her phone, tapped the screen a few times, and showed it Juliana and Rachel. "You can study peacemaking in university. I found this program in peace and conflict studies." She passed her phone to Juliana, who then read the web page a little. It was indeed a university program about dealing with conflict and trying to establish peace in the world.

Juliana raised her eyebrows in surprise. "I didn't even know that existed. You'd be absolutely perfect for that. You're level-headed, smart, and people really trust you."

Sophie blushed at the compliments.

Juliana pulled up Elisabeth's wedding photo on her phone. "I wonder if he was trying something like that—trying to fight for peace—when he died. Just look at the smile on his face…" She held up her phone to Rachel and then passed it to Sophie who enlarged the photo so she could see it better. "No way he was mean to anyone."

"And her smile," Sophie said after scrolling over a little. She then passed the phone back to Juliana, who showed the photo to Rachel again. "She looks so happy in this photo."

"But at least she moved in with her sister and Georg's wife, right?" Rachel asked. "I guess her sister never married? And we know what happened to Georg."

Juliana nodded. "From what Opa's told me these past few months, extended families lived together, like Mom, Dad, Opa, and I are right now. Maybe that's why she went back without her partner: to be with family again." She pulled up the photo with Elisabeth, a young Opa who looked maybe seven or eight years old, a woman he'd called Tante Anna, and Eva. Tante Anna had short hair and didn't wear anything to cover her head. Her dress looked modern for the '50s. Elisabeth wore what looked like an everyday kerchief to hold her hair back, pants and maybe a long-sleeved T-shirt or a thin sweater. Eva appeared in more traditional dress—a dark skirt, though it went to below her knees instead of almost to her ankle, and a dark blouse. Her kerchief still covered all her hair except for her bangs.

Juliana continued, "I'm learning that expecting my life to turn out the way I imagine it is unrealistic. I mean, look at what I learned from the interviews." Juliana listed what Pauline, Mr. Casimiro, and Tracy had all taught her. "Then there's Dad: although he's still in the same industry, he changed to an office job so he could be around more. And Mom wanted a career in dance, maybe teaching, at first. But once she began enjoying her evenings off, she changed her mind, too."

They returned their dishes to the counter, thanked Tracy for the treats again, and headed for the door.

"And you," Rachel said. "You and I were going to grow up together and be best friends forever."

"But I wouldn't have met either of you if Juliana had never moved here," Sophie said.

"And I wouldn't have met you," Juliana said to her. "But then there's Opa: his changes aren't that great."

The girls stepped outside into the bright sunlight as all the realizations sank in.

Opa's changes would indeed worsen over time. He would forget more. Some of his old—and hurtful—beliefs might return, especially the ones about Uncle Peter. The more Juliana read about Alzheimer's the more scared she became about what might come.

"Which means," Juliana continued, taking a deep breath, "change is sometimes good and sometimes bad. So, the best thing I can do is get used to it."

Rachel and Sophie burst out laughing.

Juliana crossed her arms. "I just said something groundbreaking, and now you're laughing at me?"

Rachel hugged her best friend. "It's because we know you so well. We know you're going to start planning what changes will happen."

Sophie wrapped her arms around both. "Rachel and I have only known each other for a week, and we're already in sync with you."

Juliana couldn't help but laugh, too. They were right.

But now she had her sights set on her next milestone in life: hugging a mascot. She just hadn't told Rachel and Sophie in case she chickened out. But since this week had been all about accepting change—and changing along with it—she might as well finish with this one little challenge.

Today was some of kind of sale day at Claire's Tea Shop. As expected, the giant purple cat—Pauline—was standing outside in the summer heat, high-fiving people, giving out free samples, and accepting hugs from anyone who wanted to give one.

"Let's go." Juliana walked in the cat's direction.

"Wait, what?" Rachel touched Juliana's forehead. "Are you okay?"

Sophie grabbed Juliana's wrist and pretended to take her pulse. "I don't detect any erratic heart issues."

Rachel squinted as she stared into Juliana's eyes. "Pupils appear healthy."

Juliana laughed again. "You two! I don't mind *that* mascot. Others might creep me out a bit still, but I'm good with that one."

They walked a few stores over, and after the small family ahead of them entered the store, Juliana held out her arms. "I need to say a big thank you!"

The purple cat wrapped its arms around her.

"My paper was awesome, thanks to you." She stepped back from Pauline. "It's great to live in a community like this."

Pauline held up her hand—her paw—for a high-five, and Juliana accepted.

"My plane leaves from Toronto early this evening," Rachel said. Pauline tilted her head to the side and clasped her hands near her heart. "It was so great to meet you. And thanks for everything." She hugged the cat, too.

"I just want a hug," Sophie said, and no one questioned her.

They all waved goodbye as they returned to Juliana's house. It was time.

Fifteen minutes later, Rachel and her father, Rhys, were

getting into the car. Juliana was smiling and crying at the same time. This week with Rachel had turned out even more special than she had imagined.

Rachel sprung out of the front seat again to give both girls one last hug.

"Wherever Juliana and I study, Sophie, we'll be keeping a room free for you."

"Even if it's on Prince Edward Island?"

Juliana answered. "Even if it's in the Yukon. But hopefully, we'll get together again before then."

CHAPTER EIGHTEEN

Only Anna was in the front room with Elisabeth while her family—including Tata—set up the back room and cleaned the kitchen. Elisabeth felt relief at not having to rush for maybe the first time in her life.

Anna stood on a chair to brush Elisabeth's long blonde hair.

"Are you nervous?" she asked her older sister.

"I don't think Jesus was this nervous when He fed five thousand men." Elisabeth was referring to the story in the Bible where Jesus fed five thousand men from two fish and five loaves of bread. She had never figured out why he hadn't fed the women and children.

Two days ago, after Elisabeth had stood up to her father at the table, Tata had begrudgingly allowed her to accept Stefan's offer of marriage when it came.

The news had excited Elisabeth so much that she had bolted from the table and had run as fast as she could to Stefan's house.

Now Anna began forming the first braid, on the left side of Elisabeth's hair. "But please don't scream like you did at dinner when Tata said yes," she said. "That hurt my ears." Anna had become quite adept at braiding over the months and finished the left section quickly.

Elisabeth laughed at her sister's comment. She had indeed screamed at the good news.

"I promise, I won't," Elisabeth said. "Besides, I wouldn't want to scare off his parents. Although we're now engaged, we haven't told anyone yet. They might change their minds."

Only when she'd knocked on Stefan's door had she realized how unkempt she must have looked. What would his parents think? But when Frau Schäfer opened the door, Elisabeth saw Stefan sitting at their modest kitchen table. He immediately tried fixing his own appearance: he'd had his napkin tucked in his shirt, his hair had become matted to his head from the work in the fields that day, and instead of the polished boots he'd worn to church on Sunday, he wore his house shoes.

Elisabeth could see he had a hole in the heel of one of his socks.

Now Anna passed the left braid to Elisabeth to hold

and began the one on the right. "I don't know if I ever want to marry."

"Why not? How will you have children?"

Anna brought both side braids to the middle and wove them into the single long braid she made with the rest of Elisabeth's hair. "I don't want children." She stepped down from the chair to finish the braid.

Elisabeth made eye contact with her sister through the looking glass. "But that's what women do, Anna." She handed her sister the red ribbon needed to tie the braid at the bottom.

"I don't think they all do. Do you remember that magazine Maria showed you?"

She meant the magazine from America that Maria's relative had mailed to her a few months before. "Yes."

Anna tied the bow at the bottom, and Elisabeth turned around to face her sister.

"A lot of those women weren't with men," Anna said. "And they still looked happy. I can tell that Maria won't be happy in her marriage—she doesn't smile as brightly when she's around Hagel Konrad. I think Mammi felt sad when Tata told her she can't continue her shoe business. And then it was not nice watching you hope for Tata to allow you to marry Stefan. Tata should have just said yes."

"I fought for the man I want to marry, and I will help you do the same."

Anna shook her head. "I want to move to the city. Maybe go to school."

The declaration didn't surprise Elisabeth, despite its unusualness. Anna had wanted to study math over the summer.

"But won't you miss home? And how will you pay for that? If you stay here and marry someone, he'll look after you."

Anna shook her head. "He'll want me to have children, and I don't want to look after them. I see how much you've learned—you read the encyclopedia when Mammi wasn't looking, learned how to drive a wagon, found ways to help Georg. But that took you a long time. If I go to school, I can learn faster. When Tata told us about radios in America, and electricity that keeps light on all the time...if I had those things, which I can have in Temeswar, I can learn more."

"Temeswar?" The thought of a sister living eighty kilometres away tugged at Elisabeth's heart.

"That's where the schools are."

Elisabeth hugged her younger sister. "I don't think Stefan and I will ever earn much. But if we can help you in any way, always ask." She pulled back. "That's what family is for."

Over Anna's shoulder and through the window, she caught sight of Stefan's family walking toward their house.

She immediately turned to face the looking glass again. She wore her blue-green cashmere skirt, supported by seven underskirts, and her linen blouse with its beautiful embroidery. "Do I look all right?" She tried smoothing down a few wisps of hair.

"You look beautiful, Lissika."

A knock on the side door told Elisabeth she had no more time to prepare herself should she even need it. She nervously entered the kitchen to see Stefan, his boots polished, clothing impeccably clean, step inside.

He beamed the moment he laid eyes on Elisabeth, and she couldn't help but smile just as much.

"Lissika, stop it," Mammi said. "You look stupid."

Rosina parked her hands on her hips—like a small Mammi—and said, "She looks very smart."

Everyone laughed, and even Mammi allowed the corners of her mouth to curl up.

Tata invited the Schäfers to the back room, where Elisabeth's family had laid out a magnificent supper. Everyone filed in ahead of the newly engaged couple.

Stefan held Elisabeth's hand and gave it a gentle squeeze.

"You fill me with wonder, Lissika."

Before Elisabeth could ask what he meant, he led them into the back room to sit down together at the table.

After some polite discussion, the conversation turned quickly to plans for their wedding in the winter.

ELISABETH AND STEFAN sat next to each other at the table outside while Tata and Luki showed Stefan's father the workshop, and Frau Schäfer and Magdalena helped Mammi and Elisabeth's sisters clean up.

Elisabeth pointed to the drawing of Georg's hands pulling off Anna's mittens. "This is what I thought might have been going through Georg's mind that day."

Stefan gently touched the edge of her drawing. "I don't know how you do it, but you've shown in such a lovely way what caused his fit. When we'd try to save someone who'd been shot, we'd pull them up by their hands, like you would do to help anyone stand up, but their hands would often slide out from our grip because they were covered in blood."

Elisabeth shuddered at the description.

"I'm sorry, Lissika. I didn't mean to—"

"Keep telling me," she said. "I insist. It's the only way I can understand what all of you went through."

Stefan laid his hand softly on her forearm. "If only half the people of this village could see your drawings, life for everyone would be so much easier." Elisabeth blushed and turned her gaze away. "They would understand the struggles that people like Georg have."

"But you have terrible dreams, too, don't you?"

Stefan nodded. "I don't say anything because, to me,

words make them real." He turned to the next page. "What else have you drawn?"

She showed him the next few pages, and Stefan asked her to stop at a drawing of the inside of the church before her confirmation ceremony. "You even captured all the flowers."

"It would be so nice to have our wedding in the late spring, when the first flowers have grown to their full height."

"It would be beautiful." Stefan smiled. "But I don't think anyone would come because they'd be busy tilling and preparing the fields."

Elisabeth sadly had to admit he was right.

"And I don't want to wait that long either," he said.

Tata, Luki, and Herr Schäfer passed by them. "We're about to leave," Herr Schäfer said to his son. "Will you be staying much longer? We don't want to intrude on the Schumachers' time."

"I'll be ready soon, Tata," Stefan said.

Elisabeth's father offered Herr Schäfer a quick schnapps inside, which was accepted.

Elisabeth showed Stefan the rest of her drawings, and each compliment he gave her made her blush, she was sure of it.

Once they reached the end, Elisabeth let out a long sigh. "Tata wanted me to record everything that's happened since he left, but he's never asked to see my book. Even now. Why?"

Stefan carefully closed the book. "You understand people so well, Lissika, but maybe you haven't learned this part yet. We men don't talk about how we feel with others."

"You do. That's why I wanted to marry you."

Stefan blushed. "I learned during the war that telling others a little about how I felt helped me: my friends would encourage me sometimes, or they'd help protect me in the camp if I was hurt. I also had to learn to talk about feelings as I got to know Georg: it was the only way to help him. But most men—like your father—don't do that. You said your father regrets his journey?"

Elisabeth nodded. "He regrets missing his brother's funeral. He was angry when I told him Georg had taught me how to drive a wagon. And I couldn't believe how upset he was when he learned I'd read about...babies and women's bodies...to help Mammi."

Stefan set his cap on his knee and ran his fingers through his hair. He swallowed and looked away for a moment. "He probably sees your pictures as a reminder of everything that had happened while he was gone." He captured her gaze, his eyes sad but hopeful. "But that doesn't mean you should stop drawing. Put this book somewhere safe when it's finished. You'll want your children, grandchildren, and even great-grandchildren to see it."

Her great-grandchildren? Elisabeth had never thought about anyone except Tata seeing these drawings. "Will they think these are good enough? Maybe I should buy coloured pencils. But we don't have money for that."

Stefan placed his cap back on his head, stood up from the table, and held out his hand to help her up. "They will love seeing how you lived. Hopefully, once we're married, you'll continue drawing, showing them our life together as a family, too." He walked with her to the gate, meeting up with his parents.

He doffed his cap one more time. "We'll see you in church tomorrow."

Elisabeth couldn't wait.

Jesus, can You please make Pastor Fröhlich talk faster?

Jesus, can You please tell that boy who keeps taking the organist's sheet music to stop so the music plays sooner?

Jesus, can You please push everyone out of here?

Elisabeth did ask for forgiveness throughout the service, too, but she wanted to share the news with everyone.

As usual, Jesus didn't appear to have heard her, and Pastor Fröhlich seemed to talk slower during his sermon than a cow walks.

When the service was finally over, Elisabeth's insides were bursting. She had to tell someone the good news.

Right now!

She leaned over to Maria and whispered that she and Stefan had now become engaged. Maria shrieked, drawing all eyes to her.

"Shhh!!!" Elisabeth said, laughing. "I don't need everyone else to know!"

"Know what?" one of the other girls said.

"Nothing you need to know," Maria replied. "Stop being so nosy."

The girl lifted her nose in the air in response.

Elisabeth squeezed Maria's shoulders and darted from her spot with the other *großbuben* and *großmädchen* and rushed—sometimes pushed—her way through the small crowd to Stefan's side.

Murmurs began faster than Jesus could multiply the fish and bread.

Georg, holding Little Konrad, spoke softly. "I don't think you have to worry about saying anything. Your actions have told the whole congregation."

Elisabeth, panicked, glanced around her. Georg was right: lots of smiles, some scowls, and more murmuring to one another told her she had just become the topic of conversation.

Mammi grabbed Elisabeth by the arm and pulled her

aside. Through gritted teeth, she said, "You are about to marry. Act like a woman!"

But Elisabeth didn't care: her life's dream had come true. She pulled away from her mother, and she and Stefan were immediately engulfed by hugs and handshakes at the happy news.

Maybe God and Jesus had been listening after all.

CHAPTER NINETEEN

Juliana sat in the small kitchen, her laptop on the table. She usually preferred to work in her bedroom, but without Rachel on the bed chatting away with her, it seemed so empty.

The rumble of the lawnmower outside told her that Dad was cutting the grass. Mom had to work, even though it was Sunday.

Juliana had erased her first draft and re-organized most of her notes into a new outline. Each interview shared similar themes with the others that she hadn't noticed while writing her first draft: dreams, plans, reality, change. The pattern repeated itself several times for each person.

Pauline got arthritis in her hip, Juliana wrote. *Because she was living her dream—entertaining thousands, helping just as many—she didn't want to find out what was wrong with her hip.*

"No. Too repetitive."

Pauline developed arthritis in her hip. Because she was living her dream by entertaining and helping thousands of people, she ignored the growing pain.

Juliana felt more satisfied with that sentence.

The creaking of the stairs signalled that Opa was coming up.

"You're working on a Sunday? Working is good, but everyone needs to take a pause." He tapped her gently on the shoulder and opened the fridge door.

"Homework is homework, Opa," she said. "Besides, I spent so much time with Rachel and Sophie that I need to catch up. My report is due tomorrow."

Opa placed a bag of white bread, a container of margarine, and some sliced cheese on the counter. Now that he had a small version of his photo in his pocket, copies of the originals in picture frames, and the originals themselves safely stored in the photo albums Uncle Peter had bought, Opa had a smile on his face more often.

While Opa made his sandwich, Juliana continued typing.

Pauline ignored the pain in her hip for a long time, which she said in our interview was a stupid thing to do. Because of how daring her work was, she could have broken her hip during a stunt. Or even died! So, she finally saw a doctor and eventually had her hip replaced. Pauline said that it was hard to get used to having a new hip, like not being able to go jogging anymore. But now she bicycles, and she still lifts weights.

What happened because Juliana had ignored her emotional pain for so many months? A panic attack, bouts of anger. Dance had helped her learn how to deal with her emotions.

Opa leaned over Juliana's shoulder, and she moved aside so he could read what she'd written.

"Pauline? Is that the young woman in the tea shop now?"

Young was definitely relative: Juliana thought she was *older*. "Yes. She was really nice and answered a lot of questions for my school project."

Opa continued reading. "So young and already a hip replacement. I still have both of mine." He shook his head. "What doctors can do today. If only they can replace my brain." He sat down and began eating.

Juliana considered what her grandfather had said. "But when you think about it, Opa, that would mean you'd be a different person. Who you are is in your head."

"And your heart," he added as he chewed. "Some people have small hearts. Some people have big hearts. You have a big heart, Yulika. A very big heart."

Juliana swallowed. Given how angry she'd been, especially at her parents, this past year, she didn't feel like she had a big heart.

Juliana noticed that her grandfather didn't have anything to drink. "Opa, can I get you some juice or water?"

He patted her on the shoulder again. "See? You have a big heart." He asked for a glass of orange juice.

How did offering someone a drink mean they had a big heart? To Juliana, making sure her grandfather was eating and drinking well was simply a normal thing to do.

Then she thought back to Pauline, who'd offered free tea and a snack. And Tracy, who'd done the same. Mr. Casimiro, too.

Providing her, Rachel, and Sophie something to eat and drink while Juliana asked them questions had made her feel welcome. All three business owners didn't have to offer their hospitality in that way: they were helping Juliana, not the other way around.

Juliana handed Opa his glass of juice, and he smiled as he thanked her.

A smile. That was all Juliana needed to know she'd helped someone, no matter how small the task. How often had she, Rachel, and Sophie laughed together? Or tried to cheer one another up? Juliana also thought back to when Rachel had opened her heart to encourage Sophie to be herself.

She sat down again at her laptop and typed out an idea before she forgot it.

Although Pauline's career changed—she now runs her

mother's tea shop—one thing hasn't changed: she always tries to make people smile.

Juliana had noticed that Tracy and Mr. Casimiro did the same. He'd even said the first day Juliana, Rachel, and Sophie had eaten there that he and his wife opened a restaurant because she could cook and he was friendly.

Juliana smiled to herself. That sounded like Mrs. Casimiro wasn't friendly, which was probably not what Mr. Casimiro had meant.

"Opa, did your mother try to make people smile?"

He gulped down his orange juice. "Always. She invited people over for dinner, listened to friends when they were sad or angry, and she always made sure I had clean clothes, good food, and my family."

Juliana thought back to tap class a few days ago. She had decided then and there to make as many good memories with Opa as she could.

"Opa? Can I ask you more about Omama?"

"It makes me happy that you want to know more about her."

She opened Elisabeth's book to the drawing of the house. "Is this what her house looked like?"

Opa wiped his hands on the tablecloth before turning the book to face him. "Yes. But when I grew up there, it looked different. It had a roof made from shingles, not hay. It also looked more...what's the English word...not straight." He pointed to one side of the house. "This looked low."

"I'm afraid I don't understand."

Opa carried his plate to the sink. "To make a wall for the old houses, hard clay was...what's the word?" He pressed his hands together. "It was pressed between boards of wood and then put up... But big boards of wood, not little hands. To make walls. So when the walls got old enough, they went down."

"'Went down' as in collapsed?"

Opa laughed and shook his head. "They got shorter."

Juliana was having a hard time picturing this.

"Ah! Crooked," Opa said. "Like teeth." Then he laughed his jovial laugh, and Juliana joined in.

"But how did they stay up?"

Opa shrugged. "Sometimes, you don't think about things. Even without roof damage." He pointed to his head and laughed again. "But the houses were torn down over time, so now Semlak has modern houses."

"So your old house is no longer there?"

Opa shook his head. "They're much better houses—like mine here. When I learned that our family house was gone after I moved to Canada with your grandmother, I never wanted to go back. I had nothing to go back to." He walked toward the stairs. "War hurts people. It doesn't matter where they live. But Canada is my home now."

Juliana quickly typed more notes in her report.

Opa shook his head in amazement. "Your fingers move really fast!"

"You've given me some really good ideas for my report."

Opa smiled, and the smile told Juliana that she had made him happy again. "You're working very hard. I'll leave you alone."

Juliana wanted to talk to him some more, but her brain was on fire, and she needed to get the ideas out of her head as fast as her feet could dance.

Juliana drafted the beginning to her report:

My family is used to big changes.

I grew up in a house with my parents in Calgary, but last Christmas I had to move with my parents into my grandfather's home in Kitchener. It was hard at first, but that was because my grandfather is going through a big change, too: he has Alzheimer's.

I also learned about his mother, who lived through two world wars and a political system called communism. She had to deal with a lot of big changes, too.

She added a few more sentences, then sat back and reread what she'd just written. "Those last sentences are probably better for the conclusion," she said to herself, and moved them to the end. Now, all she had to do was write the middle.

She brushed her hand over the cover of Elisabeth's notebook. Whatever the true story was behind each of those drawings, Juliana believed in her heart that they were somehow all about change because Elisabeth had tried to capture something important to her in that moment.

Within a few hours, she had her full report drafted. Juliana lifted Elisabeth's book to her heart. "I guess we don't always know what changes will come our way, do we?"

She reread her conclusion, felt satisfied with it, and stepped away from her laptop to take a pause, as Opa had instructed her to.

I was happy when I met the people for this report, who taught me how to deal with big changes as I grow up and find a career for myself. We can't avoid change. I love to plan because I like to know what's coming next. Change scares me. But now that I know it will *happen, I can plan for it.*

SETTING THE RECORD STRAIGHT

Between Worlds tells a contemporary fictional story together with a story that is historical fiction. In both parts of the book, I've taken facts about life in the time period in which the story is set and included them in a fictional story. In writing novels, the story always comes first (because otherwise this would be a history textbook), so this section explains any important facts that may have been changed to fit the story and adds more background. If you have any questions about what you've read in this, or in any of the other books in the series, ask away! My contact information is in the "Stay in Touch!" section.

HOW MANY DID JESUS FEED?

I grew up Catholic. In grade four, I was given—as per custom in the Catholic school system in Ontario—a Bible. In the almost forty years since, I've taken an interest in the cultural side of this ancient book and its translations.

One of the most well-known stories in the Bible is how Jesus fed five thousand people. However, when I researched this story for an earlier *Between Worlds* book, exactly whom Jesus fed changed. For this series, I usually referred to the King James Bible for longer passages because I understand it's the most common version of the Bible used by English-speaking Lutherans. Although I speak German and have translated in the past, translating longer passages from Luther's Bible requires cultural and linguistic knowledge I simply don't have. I can translate a few sentences, though, when needed.

This biblical story exists in two of the Gospels in both Bibles: Matthew and Mark. In the King James versions, the story ends like this:

Matthew Chapter 14: And they that had eaten were about five thousand men, besides women and children.

Mark Chapter 6: And when he had taken the five loaves and the two fishes, he looked up to heaven, and blessed, and brake the loaves, and gave them to his disci-

ples to set before them; and the two fishes divided he among them all. And they did all eat, and were filled.

When I read Luther's Bible, the story ends thus (my translation):

Matthes Chapter 14: Those, however, who had eaten were five thousand men without wives and children.
Markus Chapter 6: And those who ate there were five thousand men.

So in Elisabeth's final chapter, I returned to this biblical story to show that Elisabeth sees that some things in the Bible don't make sense—indeed, she questions her faith often throughout the series—but that she also accepts them. In her mind, the world just works that way.

"EXPERIENCE" BY LUDUVICO EINAUDI

I discovered composer Luduvico Einaudi maybe ten years ago, and I've come to enjoy his music. You may have seen an online video of a man playing the piano on an ice floe. (An ice floe can best be described as a thick sheet of floating ice.) That is Einaudi. I wanted to include one of his songs in this last novel. You should be able to find it on any legal streaming source.

EPILEPSY

Epilepsy is a condition I live with, and it comes in many forms. Mine is a rare type of absence seizure syndrome called epilepsy with eyelid myoclonia. In layperson's terms, I have seizures that may or may not be visible, and my eyelids will flicker, but not always with a seizure. I don't collapse, nor do my muscles jerk. Often, people I'm speaking with don't even know I've had one.

Austin's seizures cause what some refer to as staring spells. These are also absence seizures. Most people with absence seizures lead a fairly normal life. However, some may not be able to drive or operate heavy machinery if their seizures are not controlled. Austin's journey from diagnosis to acceptance is the topic of my next young adult series. Keep an eye out for it!

THE LAST NOVEL

This marks my last novel in this series. Thank you for joining Juliana and Elisabeth on their journeys. I would love to hear what you thought about it! My contact information is in the "Stay in Touch!" section.

STAY IN TOUCH!

If you enjoyed the book, sign up for my monthly newsletter! I write it myself, so it's my words to you. You'll get the following:

- Sneak peeks at upcoming books
- Updates about online and in-person appearances
- Book and writing recommendations
- Recipes I love
- Contests
- And more!

Visit BetweenWorldsYA.com to sign up!

Prefer social media? All my links are listed under my bio, at the end of the book.

COLLECT ALL THE BOOKS IN THE SERIES

Don't miss out on a single step in Juliana's and Elisabeth's journeys. You can order the books below from your favourite book store or online retailer.

AVAILABLE IN REGULAR PRINT, LARGE PRINT, AND EBOOK

1. The Move
2. The Distance
3. The First Step
4. What Friends Do
5. Hide and Seek
6. Missing Home
7. What Will Come
8. A Father's Journey
9. Rhythms Shared

Also check out my blog for more background information about the series. You'll read about some of the research that went into the book, discover more about the real Canadian neighbourhoods used in the book, and learn about writing. Visit www. BetweenWorldsYA.com.

ACKNOWLEDGMENTS

This *series* would not have been possible without the help of so many people.

For research:

- Georg Schmidt and the HOG Semlak (semlak.de)
- Anne Dreer, Rose Mary Keller Hughes, Mrs. Rossweiler, and the members and organizers of Donauschwaben Villages Helping Hands
- Romanian researchers Crenguta Nicolae, Gabriela Rat, Daniel Kalman, and Levente Csibi
- High school teachers Annamae Elliott and Erika Werner, and St. Mary's High School vice principal Deanna Wehrle
- Sara Marsh, who shared with me stories of growing up with a father who drove trucks for his career
- Retired Lutheran pastor Henry A. Fischer

- School of Optometry and Vision Sciences at the
  University of Waterloo
- Former workers of our local rubber factories

For mentorship:

- Heather Wright
- ali macgee

For dance training:

- Deardra King-Leslie
- Beth Krug
- Sharon Laramie
- April March
- All the student teachers who taught me when I
  was really young

For publication:

- Susan Fish
- Jennifer Dinsmore
- Michelle Fairbanks
- Phoebe Wolfe (with an *e*)
- Kyle Bergum

And last, my family: Mom and Dad, my sister's family,

and Corey, Khristopher, and Jonnathan. Thank you for continuing to encourage and support me for the seven years it took to write and publish this series.

This has been a journey. I can't wait for the next one to begin.

ABOUT LORI

Photo by Erin Watt Photography

Lori Wolf-Heffner is a former competitive dancer, dance teacher, and theatre manager. She was a member of the first Canadian National Tap Team, back in 1996, under the leadership of Bonnie Dyer, with choreographer Mathew Clark. She's written for *Dance Canada Quarterly*, *just dance!* magazine, and *The Dance Current* (all under Lori Straus).

Fluent in German, Lori lived in Germany for three years, never once realizing just how close she was to some of the villages her ancestors left to migrate to Eastern Europe in the 1700s.

Lori lives in Waterloo, Ontario, Canada, with her husband and two sons. She is a member of The Writers' Union of Canada and the Alliance of Independent Authors.

facebook.com/loriwolfheffner

instagram.com/loriwolfheffner

goodreads.com/lori_wolf-heffner

bookbub.com/author/lori-wolf-heffner

pinterest.com/loriwolfheffner

amazon.com/author/loriwolfheffner

www.ingramcontent.com/pod-product-compliance
Lightning Source LLC
Chambersburg PA
CBHW061349310726
48974CB00001B/264